Forbidden Passion

Historic-Romance

XXX, Adult Content, War, Peace, and

Elizabeth "Liz" Fleming

Best Wishes

Forbidden Passion

Civil War Era Love Affairs

Forbidden Passion

BY: Lucy Elizabeth "Liz" Fleming

Historic-Romance

Published May 14, 2014

First Edition

Copyright by Dahnmon Whitt Family Publishing

P.O. Box 831 Flatwoods, KY. 41139 Phone 606 836 7997

ISBN 978-1-63068-481-5

9 781630 684815

Contents

Chapter	Page

Chapter   Page

Preface

This book is a good account of the War of Northern Aggression as well as a nineteenth century romance novel.

Liz Fleming does a good job with her historic facts and then blends in a surprising exotic display of hot sex.

The characters are surprising and reflect the era of the Great War. We see the conflict of war in the mind-sets of the people.

Liz also brings out the conflict between two beautiful redheads that want the same man.

Liz does a good job of putting people and even things in the Civil War era.

There is mention of slaves and I think it is portrayed accurately.

The Nation was divided mostly in politics at first, then by guns, blood, and grief.

There is another slant on President Abraham Lincoln.

There is also a look at the rag-tag Confederate Army that in spite of overwhelming odds; held back the might of the Union Army for four long years.

Chapter 1

Colonel Alexander Phipps

This is a story of love and passion in another time and place. The time was in the spring of 1861.

Rendition of Colonel Alexander Phipps

Don Strivers Art

 It is about unlikely meetings and powerful attractions. It was also a time of great discord.

During the War of Northern Aggression, a man from the south meets a northern lady, all by accident and things take off from there.

Let us meet Colonel Alexander Phipps of the staff of General Robert E. Lee. His job is to make contact with spies and use other forms of intelligence gathering. The

Colonel is a young single man with the ambition to go far in the Army of the Confederacy. He came from a well to do family and was able to get an appointment to Virginia Military Institute. The Colonel has never allowed time for courtship or even meeting eligible ladies, not that he was not all man. In his young life, he has heard many stories of ways to woo a woman and give her complete pleasure yet he has been devoted to his military career and put all his energy into it.

Colonel Phipps was always well dressed either in uniform or in Southern Gentleman attire. When the circumstances called for it, he would wear clothes of a poor northern man to make contact with spy connections.

Early in the war, Colonel Phipps was sent north to meet some informers. These informers were from Hagerstown, Maryland and well to do families but had a strong desire to help the southern states win their war of Independence.

Now I think we all know that spying is a very dangerous thing to do during wartime. It carries the decree of traitor and the death sentence.

This trip the Colonel would wear his fine civilian clothing and hoped to meet the standards of dress of the family he would meet with. The Colonel would ride his thoroughbred steed and travel as a businessman. He had to be careful not to draw attention to himself. His southern drawl was close to that in southern Maryland.

Forbidden Passion

The Wellington family with southern sympathies was well regarded and not suspected. This family held frequent parties and balls. The ladies of the family were always holding teas for the ladies of the area.

Now all the young ladies frequented the cotillions and teas as their main social affairs. There was a beautiful lady of nineteen with long curled red hair. She was quiet and reserved, but loved the social gatherings. This beautiful young lady's name was Henrietta Adams. Henrietta was true to the Union as Colonel Phipps was loyal to the Confederacy.

Colonel Alexander Phipps had made plans to visit the Wellingtons at one of their well-attended balls. This would take away from suspicions by nosy northerners. Alexander Phipps would join in at the party and have a private meeting with Thomas Wellington for brandy and smoking. The gentlemen of the time loved to talk while they smoked their pipes or cigars. Therefore, this planned meeting would be ordinary and no one would really notice.

The only thing that would throw the young colonel was the presence of the red haired beauty, Henrietta Adams.

Colonel Phipps was at the Wellington Home in time to have the stable help take care of his beautiful horse, Prancer. The Negroes at the barn were happy to see such a grand horse and went on something terrible about the grand animal. Colonel Phipps spoke kindly to the Negroes and said, please take care of Prancer for me... "Oh, yes Sir we will treat Mister Prancer mighty kindly."

Colonel Phipps told the stable men to give him plenty of food and water and to curry him down. The Negroes smiled widely and acknowledged the Colonels remark with a big, "Yes Sir Master Phipps." Colonel Phipps petted Prancer on the flank and smiled at the Negroes, then headed to the front door of the Wellington House. He was greeted at the door by a well-dressed "house nigger," as they were called with no prejudices.

"Come in Sir, let me take your hat and I will announce you to Master Wellington," said the servant.

The Colonel gave the black servant his hat and walked over to the cold fireplace to wait. The mantle was well decorated with family pictures and some small paintings of the family members.

The Colonel was aware of this well to do family and knew that John Wellington would help the cause of the Confederacy as much as he possible could without jeopardizing his position as a northerner.

Colonel Phipps was expecting a big dominate man, but John Wellington entered the room as a small well-dressed man, but with great confidence.

The older Wellington took the hand of Colonel Phipps and gave him a hardy southern handshake.

"Welcome to my home Mister Phipps," said the master of the plantation.

8

"Thank you sir, I am so glad to make your acquaintance," said the Colonel.

After the pleasantries were over John Wellington called for a servant to show the Colonel to an upstairs room to rest and freshen up before dinner.

Colonel Phipps followed the Negro carrying his saddlebags and a traveling sack up the spiral staircase.

The Colonel had seen homes with this much splendor, but not many. Then his thoughts went back to his mission. He was wondering what secrets he would learn that may help General Lee expel the invading Yankee army.

After the Colonel went into his room, the Negro asked, "Sir, wills there be anything else I can hep you with, afore dinner?"

"No, I am fine you go about your business," answered the Colonel. The Negro left the room and closed the door behind him.

Later about 5 O'clock, there was a knock on the Colonel's door.

"Yes," answered the Colonel.

"Dinner is served, Master Phipps.," said the Negro.

"I shall be right down," answered the Colonel.

After the Colonel was seated with the family, the house servants served the meal and the family said little as they dined. After dinner, John Wellington took Colonel Phipps to the porch to smoke. He politely ask questions about the Colonel's family and had pleasant small talk. He told the Colonel the guests would be arriving soon for the cotillion.

John Wellington told the Colonel in a low voice that he wanted to have brandy and smokes after the ball and had some information for him. The Colonel seemed anxious as he nodded that he understood.

Rendition of Henrietta, (Hannah) Wright, Adams

Chapter 2

Henrietta Adams

The evening passed and the guest started arriving for the festivities.

After some, dancing and more talking Alexander sits with Hannah. Alex discourages other young men from taking his new friend to the dance floor. Some did succeed but not many. The evening passed fast and Alexander learned that Henrietta was from a large family and was not as proper with him now that they had spent time together.

Henrietta talked with Alexander most of the evening and let him know that her best friends called her "Hannah," and he could if he liked.

Alexander let her know that friends often called him Alex and he would enjoy her calling him the more informal name. They had hit it off quite well and they danced so well together. Both from well to do families they both had experience on the dance floor.

Now in the era of the war men and women kept a good distance from each other while dancing and never touched as dancers do today. However, they seemed to bump together often, breast to chest, Hannah was a bit forward and on the naughty side. Of course, their hands touch often as he helped her rise from her chair or any other time they could touch without drawing attention.

Y'all know that hand touching can be a way for the electricity to pass from one lover to another and they both felt the current.

Alex asked Hannah if he might call on her while he was in the Hagerstown area. Moreover, of course he could as long it was handled proper and the permission of her father was given.

Time for the ball to end and guests were told good-bye and Alex had to let Hannah go. He wondered if he was out of his mind, being so attracted to a Union minded woman. However, she was so pretty and they both had felt the attractions so deeply.

Hannah left with a brother and another lady for home and they said volumes with their eyes at her last glance at Alex.

When Hannah got home, she reflected on the night and knew that Alex was very special. She noticed when she undressed, that she was quite damp.

The seed of love had been planted and the love bug had struck both Hannah and Alex!

Chapter 3

The Mission

The house got quiet as the folks were gone and the servants quietly went about their business of cleaning up and putting furniture back into its place.

Alexander Phipps is stunned as he reflects on the evening. What happened he asked himself?

John Wellington came to Alex and ask him to join him for brandy and a cigar. Alex followed John up the spiral staircase to the upper porch where they could talk in private.

John looked at Alex and asked, "Alex, do you know what you are doing getting that close to a strong Union supporter?"

"Well Sir, it just kinda happened, it might even be good cover for me making trips to Hagerstown," said Alex.

"You may have a point, son, I never looked at it that way," said John Wellington.

Both men sat with a brandy and lit up a nice cigar and the talk began.

John tells the young Colonel of General McClellan's plans that he has learned from deep inside the Lincoln's Administration.

Forbidden Passion

Big secret news, General McClellan has a big army and is going to try an invasion by the peninsular. The Confederate Army will have notice and will be able to counter the bigger Union army. McClellan is a very cautious commander and the Confederates make him think he is outnumbered.

This information that Colonel Alexander Phipps brought will save the Confederacy, at least for now was their thinking. In March, the Peninsula Campaign begins as McClellan's Army of the Potomac advances from Washington down the Potomac River and the Chesapeake Bay to the peninsular south of the Confederate Capital of Richmond, Virginia then begins an advance toward Richmond.

The Army of Northern Virginia used trickery and made McClellan too cautious to do the Confederacy any great harm. The use of "Quaker Cannons" and the action of a smaller army by much demonstration and flag waving scared the Union Commander. Quaker Cannons are mere logs painted black and stuck up to appear to be cannon.

With the advanced news the Confederates out do the Union army, even the daring J.E.B. Stuart Calvary commander rides all the way around the Union Army and made headlines in both the southern and northern newspapers.

Even President Jefferson Davis praises Colonel Alexander Phipps. He will have a few weeks furlough and yes; he heads to Hagerstown Maryland on business...To see the beautiful Hannah. Of course, he will have his eyes and ears open to gather any information that may be of help to General Lee. The Wellingtons in Hagerstown will be visited for sure.

Hannah is so glad to see her Alexander Phipps come riding up the lane through the great oaks that had been planted there years before to shade the road and make the plantation look so welcome.

Chapter 4

Back to Hagerstown

Alex was invited to stay at the William Adams plantation on this trip at the beckoning of Hannah Adams. Mister William Adams agreed only if Alex would agree to be sewed into a bundling bag each night, as was the tradition of the times. The bundling bag was just a cotton material bag made into something resembling a sleeping bag. It was designed to protect the virginity of the young ladies of the house from a visiting gentleman. After the gentleman was ready to retire for the night, he would simply wiggle into the bag and the lady of the house would come in and sew it shut with only the gentleman's head sticking out. Then in the morning, the lady would come in and examine the stitches to ensure he had not been taken out or torn. Then she would release him by removing the stitches. He would wiggle out and be free the rest of the day.

Bedtime came at the Adams home and Alex was told to go and get ready for bed and holler when he was in the bundling bag.

Alex did as he was told and after he had wiggled into the bundling, he hollered, "I am ready, come sew me in!"

Mrs. Martha Adams came through the door grinning and she was followed closely by a smiling Hannah. Mrs.

Martha Adams had her needle threaded and had a thimble on one finger.

There was some small talk as she sewed the stitches on both sides over his shoulders. Once done only the smiling face of the captive Alex was showing. Mrs. Adams said, "There, that should keep you for the night" and smiled at Alex.

Mrs. Adams left the room so the two young people could talk and say goodnight. Hannah sat by the bed and looked into the eyes of her young man. She surprised him by quickly bending over and placing a hot wet kiss right on his mouth.

Passion rose in Alex quickly as he realized the contact of the kiss. There as he lay in the bundling bag, the excitement rushed throughout his body and there was a rising in the bag just below his waist.

Hannah noticed this bulge but said nothing but gave him a wide smile. She got up and said, "Good night Alex Phipps."

Then without any warning, Hannah reached over, gave the rising spot a tap with her palm and left the room. He had flinched a little bit and she had let out a little giggle.

Alex is laying there kinda blushing and wondering about the beautiful Hannah. Could she know more and more experience than her innocent face showed? At any rate, he was aroused and excited by her playful actions. He also let his mind wonder about her beauty and thought, wonder if all her hair is red.

Finally, after an hour or so he drifted off to sleep. He woke up to the smell of bacon frying and the sounds of busy servant making breakfast and getting things ready for the new day. He was ready to be released from his bundling bag and was thinking about going out to the family privy. He could easily break free, but thought better of it as it would cast a shadow of mischief.

He had memories of Hannah and the love tap she gave him as she left his room. Could she know he had an erection or was it a childish gesture? He thought more about it, she might be giving him something to think, she sure did succeed if that was the plan.

Alex needed to get up and go pee. He looked down and oh my there was the tent pole again. He took his hand and held it down as Mrs. Adams entered the room to release him from the bondage of the bundling bag. Of course, Hannah followed her mother into the room to see how Alex had faired the night.

Then came small talk and Mrs. Adams was gentle removing the stitches to free the captive. The talk and presence of both of the ladies was a blessing as Alex felt the tent pole was now laying down.

Mrs. Adams left the room and before Alex could think about getting out of the bundling Hannah gave a repeat of last night, she kissed his mouth again.

Then Hannah said, "Get ready for breakfast and I will see you at the table with my family," then she went out and shut the door so he could rise and dress.

Finally, Alex was able to wiggle out of the bundling bag and get dressed. He looked something like a giant butterfly emerging from the cocoon.

Alex reflected on the things that had happened between Hannah and himself. Love is brewing as well as sexual excitement. He had a strange warm feeling like a glow when he thought of Hannah. Then he would snap back to reality and his mission. Besides, she is a Damn Yankee.

Alex had plans on riding over to see the Wellingtons after breakfast. He knew that Mister John Wellington would share any information he may have about the Union's plans to attack the Confederacy.

Alex dressed and went to the family privy, after returning a black servant met him and took him to a nice warm pitcher of water and poured some in a beautiful bowl for Alex to wash up for breakfast. He washed his face as well as his hands and the servant handed him a nice clean towel. After drying, he handed the towel to the servant and said, "Thank You."

The servant gave a wide smile with his big white teeth beaming and said, "you's Welcome suh."

Alex followed his nose to the dining room where a servant that pulled out a chair for him next to Miss

Hannah. Alex took the seat and looked at Hannah; she was giving him a wonderful smile. He smiled back and said good morning to the Adams family. Mister Adams was seated at the head of the table and blessed the food.

The plates were filled and all began to eat, Alex took a nice bite of bacon and just about choked when he felt Hannah's hand on the inside of his thigh. Mister Wellington looked up to see if Alex was all right, and then went back to eating.

Somehow, she kept it up most of breakfast and kept on eating. Alex had a hard problem and she actually touched it a time or two. He was thinking, "Oh God, how will I ever get up if she don't quit?"

Was this all true, was this beautiful lady that forward, and she was so beautiful? Alex had been with some hot loose women before, yet this was different, he had both love and sex on his mind.

Alex was finally able to stand up and thank the family for their hospitality, and thought it best to go get his horse and take that ride to the Wellingtons.

The Struggle 1861 - 1865

Chapter 5

Think About What

When Alex went to the stable, a servant was there to saddle his fine riding horse. Prancer was his name and he was a tall red thoroughbred horse.

The stable man told Alex that he had taken special care of Prancer and even given him sweet oats. He said,"Suh dis here Prancer is a fine hoss, I just loves him to death!"

Alex thanked the servant and gave him a smile, as he knew this Negro knew good horseflesh.

Her mother had captured Hannah as the mother could see what was going on. "Hannah, I do need you to help me in the parlor, we have to decide on some colors for the room."

"Yes Mother," she said, moving toward the parlor reluctantly.

For now, Alex was free and ready to breathe in the fresh country air as he rode Prancer to the Wellingtons.

Once again, in his mind, Alex was Colonel Alexander Phipps. He would go about on his mission and may have to ride back south soon, but actually wanted to get back to Hannah. The Wellingtons were glad to see the Colonel but just greeted him as Alex.

"Alex, it is so good to see you again," said John Wellington.

"Thank you sir, it is my pleasure to see you and your fine family again," answered Alex.

"Come son, let us go have coffee, I want to hear about your family and your travels," said Mister Wellington.

Alex followed Mister John Wellington out to a gazebo and a servant soon arrived with tea, coffee, and fine cigars.

Mister Wellington nodded a thank you to the Negro servant and he left the two gentlemen.

The coffee was poured and the gentlemen smiled as they talked about the latest success of the Confederate Army.

Alex spoke, "Sir thank you so much for the information, you have helped our cause immensely with the information, and do you have any new reports for the war department?"

Mister John Wellington took a big draw on his fine cigar, expelled the smoke and answered, "Yes I think I do, I know General Poke has raised the Union Army numbers to 75,000 troops. I also know The Confederate Army is undermanned, but if you get this word to them, maybe a good stand at Manassas will be able to repel then again!"

"Sir this is good to know, are there any more details?" if not I must go" replied Colonel Alexander Phipps.

Mister John Wellington looked all around then smiles at Alexander, "go son get on your stead and ride and may God be with our cause."

Colonel Phipps rose and headed for the stable and Prancer was ready for a ride. After mounting his fine horse, the Colonel's first thoughts were of Hannah. Thank God, the Adams plantation is on the way, I have to see Hannah one more time before I go further south he thought.

Alex rode up to the Adams plantation and a servant took Prancer by the reigns. Alex told him to give him just a bit of water he would not tarry long and he would be on his way. Alex went to the door, but by now, Hannah knew who it was and came out of the big door to greet him.

He told Hannah that he received a message of some importance and must ride home. He told her he would return at the first opportunity.

She took him by the arm and walked him around to the side of the house where there was a bench under a great oak. She sat him down and pulled him close. He took the lead this time and pressed his lips to hers and they had a long passionate kiss. She took his hand and placed it on her breast and he felt her full hot breast through her dress. He massaged her breast as they kissed.

Finally, he rose and pulled Hannah to her feet, he pulled her close, and she let her hand dangle between them where she found his hard member and pressed the issue.

"Oh! Hannah I must leave you but please keep me in your thoughts and prayers," he said as he turned and walked to where Prancer was waiting.

Alex turned sideways to wave at Hannah and she giggles shyly as she saw he walked with a bulge in his pants.

By the time the Colonel was to Prancer, the stiffness had diminished and he got on Prancer and headed south. Now Colonel Phipps had lots to think about as he rode. He had information for the Army of Northern Virginia and that beautiful red head had him so twitterpated. Then he thought about her remarks against the Confederacy, damn, damn, what a dilemma.

This trip Colonel Phipps went right through the lines without any problem and headed to the army. Pickets met him; he showed his pass and asked to see the commanding general on duty.

This time he was escorted to General Longstreet. He reported his information and stated he saw several blue uniforms in southern Maryland.

General Longstreet sent a dispatch to General Stonewall Jackson with orders to prepare his army and head to Manassas with great haste.

General Lee was in Richmond and time was short so Longstreet and Jackson managed an army of 55,000 strong southern-minded men. In addition, forced marched to defend on Bull Run Creek one more time. By being, ready Poke and his 75,000 union boys were repelled and scampered back to Washington City one more time. This time Colonel Alexander was blessed to ride with the generals and saw the mighty 55,000 man army in action. This took place on August 29th and 30th 1862.

Now this victory sets General Lee to thinking, he should go and take back Harpers Ferry from the Federals. Some way the Federals have built their Army to 90,000 strong. McClellan has his Army ready to defend. General Lee has only 50,000 Confederates and they clash at Antietam, Maryland. Both Armies fought and the south did well but the odds was against them. General Lee withdrew and on the bloody fields lay 26,000 dead, wounded or missing. This is the most Americans ever to die in any battle.

Even though it was a tie, General Lee withdrew; Lincoln called it a great victory and used it for his purpose to issue the Emancipation Proclamation and freed the slaves. (Only in the Confederate held states.)

This was on September 22, 1862. He was careful not to free any in the border or northern states as they may jump to the aid of the Confederacy. This was pleasing to some folks and would quiet down some of the street riots going on in northern cities. Many people in the north really wanted the war over and let the Confederacy be their own country.

Once again Colonel Alexander Phipps dons his civilian suit and rides north. This time he wants to see the reaction of the northern people to the war and the Emancipation Proclamation given by Lincoln to increase the popularity of the war effort.

This time he leaves under cover of darkness and crosses through the lines undetected once again. He stops in a little town, picks up papers, and talks to several folks. He had several conflicting views as he makes his way to Hagerstown once again.

Chapter 6
Burnside Takes Charge

Lincoln is so put out with his General McClellan that he replaces him with General Burnside. Lincoln thought McClellan should have followed Lee's Army and destroy it while Lee was retreating. The Northern War machine was planning a great assault on Fredericksburg Virginia and end the war under General Burnside.

Colonel Phipps as Alex the Drummer (peddler) went to see Mister John Wellington again. In addition, he would go see the beautiful Hannah Adams as well.

Since The Adams Plantation is mostly on the way to Wellington's plantation and of course Alex wants to see Hannah so he stops to rest Prancer and see the redheaded beauty.

The Adams family are glad to see their young friend especially Hannah. After greetings and hugs, Alex is invited in for coffee and morning snacks.

Finally, Hannah and Alexander are left on their own recognizance, which might be a mistake. As soon as the room is cleared, they embrace and kiss. She pauses to tell him there is a ball at the John Wellington Plantation again and wants to go with Alex. Alex is much in favor of this, but must talk to John Wellington as soon as possible before making big plans.

Alex tells Hannah yes, but only if he is free at the time. Hannah made a face at him and he pulls her close and kisses her lips, and face even her eyes.

This time Alex takes liberties, pushes his hand down into her low cut dress, and has a hand full of hot breast. Hannah is somewhat stunned but does not resist. He even has luck to find her hot nipple and rubs it between his fingers. She has a low moan coming from her hot lips. Suddenly they here footsteps so he yanks out his hand. Someone had walked by the door and on out the main door. Hannah's face is red to match her hair at the excitement they had shared.

Alex told Hannah he would plan to escort her to the ball, but first had to take care of business. Then he rose up and by her hand, he pulled her to her feet. Once again, they kissed and once again, she felt of his hardness, this time actually gripping him the best she could through his pants.

Oh! Alex must leave and go about his business, the war is more important than even this beautiful woman. Alex withdrawals a step back and she looks at his bulge in his pants and back at him with a beautiful smile.

Alex hopes his hard problem will subside so he can walk to the stable and get his horse. He needs to go and see John Wellington.

John Wellington is out overseeing the picking and storing of his corn harvest. Alex is told where he is so he rides to the field where much activity is going on. Corn is being picked, fodder shocks are made, and the corn is loaded on big wagons to be taken to the barns and cribs.

John sees Alex coming, gives some orders to the overseer and wheels his horse. He rides to meet Alex. John tells him to follow and they go up on a high place where he can see all about and have privacy. They both dismount and greet each other with handshakes and smiles.

Colonel Alexander Phipps thanks John Wellington for all the help and he told him he saw the Yankee's behinds as they scampered back to Washington, and that General Lee was nowhere defeated even at Antietam, but was so outnumbered he did not want to lose another man so he withdrew.

John told the Colonel about Burnside taking charge and about the plan to go to Fredericksburg on a winter mission and wanted to crush the Confederacy.

"Sir how much time do you think we have before this plan goes into effect?" asked Colonel Phipps.

"I think less than a month," answered John.

"Son, I am hosting a Ball Saturday evening, I think you might want to stay and go to that," continued John Wellington.

"Thank you sir, I could use some relaxation," replied the Colonel.

John Wellington confided to Colonel Alexander Phipps that the red headed Adams lady was not a virgin. Actually, she was married to a Wright man about two years back and he had been killed tragically in a horse race. The race was just between him and a friend for bragging rights. Ben Wright was thrown from his mount, broke his neck, and died instantly.

Henrietta had mourned for a year and she lived with her family so she just assumed the Adams name again.

This explained a lot to the young Colonel.

Chapter 7

Passion rises

It is November and the evening air is cold on this November night. Folks were bundled up in their buggies and some were driven in fine carriages with a matched team of fine horses. To look about Hagerstown you would not think there was a war going on.

Alex had spent another night bundled at the Adams home. Once again, Hannah had flirted and teased him, even kissing him and feeling through the material of the bundling. Alex was wondering how a young woman like her seemed to know and want to experience sexual fantasies. Could she be a soiled dove? Whatever she is, he is aroused.

Alex had lots of time to think in his bundling and began to reason there will be a time coming, he would lay her down and give her what she wants. Could he be misreading her, he does not think so?

This evening The Adams family gave the loan of the beautiful family carriage, two black horses of high quality pulled it, and the family driver, a Negro servant would drive them to the ball.

It was time to leave and Alex helped Hannah into the carriage and he sit down close beside her. She was holding a good heavy quilt so she started opening it up.

Alex took hold of one side and helped her spread it over their legs and laps. Her hand was under the quilt and she placed it on his thigh and gave it a squeeze. Adam thought, there she goes so he put his hand on her hand and held it gently.

Alex told the driver to go and take them to the John Wellington Plantation. The driver cracked the whip, the team pulled into their harnesses, and the carriage was on its way.

The young couple snuggled together and looked at each other with hungry eyes; Hannah's hand inched further toward the inside of his thigh. This action of course caused a reaction and Alexander felt his member rising. Just before they got to the Wellington plantation, Hannah's hand actually had reached her target, and she felt the hardness of young Alex.

Alex had a problem again and would have to walk in with the bulge in his pants if it did not subside quickly. Hannah looked at him and her eyes were laughing at his problem.

Thank goodness, the November sun sets quickly, this would give Alex a better chance to walk in without everyone noticing his problem.

The ball went well and he pretty much kept Hannah to himself. They did all the dances but preferred the waltz. The Negro music players were wonderful. You could tell they did not mind playing for the white folks. These

Negros were treated extra well and at the end of the dance, they would take all the leftover food back to their families as a treat.

Alex was thinking about the ride back to the Adams plantation and knew there would be some kissing and some more touching.

The two hot-blooded young couple hurried to get the quilt over their laps and told the driver to take his time. The thought kept coming back into the Colonel's head. This hot lady is an enemy of mine. Then he would think, not tonight she is not my enemy, and back to kissing and touching. She did everything but unbutton his pants and free his hard member. He actually got his hand under her hoop and played with her upper leg through her pantaloons   but there were just too much material to get his hand where he wanted it.

As the driver drove up to the Adams home Alex held her tight and gave her a good kiss. Time to go in and get bundled again and this night Alex really want to get un-bundled but would be the gentleman he was supposed to be.

After a good night of sleep and being released from the bundling, Alex was ready to eat, say his thanks and goodbyes, and head south. He had his fun now it was back to the business of the war.

Knowing that Hannah was a Union supporter nagged at him often. Well it is just fun he would say but down deep, there was the seed of love growing daily.

Colonel Alexander was now riding Prancer and talking to him occasionally to pass the time. Prancer always seemed to hear and understand.

Now just up ahead was a column of blue coated Union Calvary heading towards him. The Young Colonels heart leaped, and he knew he had to appear calm and give his story of being a drummer.

As the Union lieutenant held up his hand and the two by two patrol halted, Colonel Alexander spoke as if relieved.

"Glad to see you boys out doing your job Major," said Alex.

"Why is that and I am a Lieutenant," answered the Union commander of the party.

"Oh, it is kinda dangerous out on the roads these days for a peddler like me," answered Alex.

"Drummer, what are you selling and where are you heading?" asked the lieutenant?

"Lots of things," Alex answered as he handed him his catalog of goods.

"Look there on page 223, you fellows could use one of those," said Alex.

The young Union officer leafed through the catalog and on page 223 was the new repeating Henry Rifle. He looked up at Alex with a smile and said, "Dang right I could use one of these and all my men, just one thing holding us back, those things cost as much as a small farm!"

Well sir I have sold a few and you can load on Sunday and shoot all week," said Alex with a big grin.

"Drummer, go your way and be careful, some gray-coats about," said the Lieutenant.

Alex bid the Yankees farewell and walks Prancer on down the road.

As soon as Colonel Alexander is out of sight of the Union patrol, he tells Prancer his sentiment, "Dammed Yankees"

Riding on the trail for another mile or so Alex sees riders coming with hast, a cloud of dust rises above the Column of men as they approach.

Alexander is thinking to himself, "Hope these guys are not more yanks."

The men in gray and the cloud of dust stop beside Colonel Alexander Phipps. He waves his hand to the mounted soldiers.

The Confederate Colonel in charge of this big Calvary troop gets straight to the matter.

"Sir, what is your name, and what is your business out on this highway?"

Colonel Alexander Phipps salutes and states his name and also says, "I am about the business of the Confederate States of America, I have papers in my boot if you will allow me to get them, Sir"

"By all means and you better be who you say you are," replied the other Colonel.

Colonel Phipps had to dismount and take off his boot, and then he pulled out an envelope with the papers. He handed them up to the Colonel to read.

Colonel Alexander Phipps is on official business for the Confederate States of America. Do not detain him for any reason!

Signed First Corps of the Army of Northern Virginia, General Longstreet

Also on the document was the seal of General Longstreet.

The Colonel of the patrol looked at him and smiled, then saluted him and said, "go about your business Sir, sorry I detained you."

Colonel Phipps saluted the other Colonel and said, "Sir it is a pleasure to see you on duty here, I passed a small patrol of Yanks bout two miles north of here."

"Yes we know we aim to run them pole cats out of our country," stated the Colonel.

Now Colonel Alexander Phipps rides Prancer a little harder, toward the main Confederate Army.

Rendition of Prancer

Chapter 8

Fredericksburg

Colonel Alexander Phipps made his way to the Army of Northern Virginia and was stopped by the pickets. After he proved to the Confederate Pickett who he was he was sent with an escort to see General Stonewall Jackson.

The General bid him come into his tent where he was reading his Bible.

"Come in Colonel, what word do you have for me today?"

I have been reading about Gideon defeating a great army with only 300 brave men. Of course, it was not Gideon; it was the hand of God that provides us our victories.

"Yes Sir, you have been very powerful with the help of almighty God," replied Colonel Phipps.

Finally, after several Bible stories about mere people obeying God had defeated great armies or had other great successes, the Colonel started giving his report.

"General Sir, Lincoln has a new commanding General, He has put Burnside in charge and he plans to come to Fredericksburg and cross over the river and march his army on to Richmond.

Burnside is following orders from the war department and will not take a step unless so ordered. In addition, it looks like his orders will put him at Fredericksburg in late November or December.

"Well a winter assault, rare for those people to try that," said General Jackson.

"I kinda thought that too sir, but my sources all agree it is coming," answered Colonel Phipps.

"Thanks Colonel, well done, excuse me and I will pray, you go out by the fire and send in the officers waiting, but give me five minutes please," commanded General Jackson.

Colonel Phipps gave a hardy salute even though he was in civilian attire, and left the General's tent. He went over to the fire where several of the General's officers were waiting and warming by the fire.

"Hello Sirs, General Jackson told me to give him a few minutes and then come inside his tent as he has news for you," said Colonel Phipps.

They knew he had just come from the Generals tent but they still looked at him funny, as he was not in uniform.

General Jackson sent speedy dispatches to General Lee and to General Longstreet with the information and left it up to General Lee to take the news and do what he thought best. General Lee did not sit on it he gathered his Army, rushed to Fredericksburg, Virginia, and

41

surveyed the grounds. Behind the town was a great field and high ground at the back. It was a natural place to place his army. The hill was called Marye's Heights and there was a great stonewall already built all the way across. It was perfect for the defense for the Army of Northern Virginia.

It was not take long before the invaders of General Burnside arrived under orders from Washington D.C. On December 13, 1862, Burnside sent in 14 different frontal attacks across the vast fields towards Marye's Heights. It was awful; The Yankee Army gave up 12,653 men to the blistering firepower coming from the Confederates. One Confederate officer remarked that even a rabbit could not live on that field. The Confederate loss was 5,309 men and most of them were killed in the town of Fredericksburg slowing the invaders crossing the river.

It was a needless loss of life in such a foray.

After looking at the carnage on the field, General Robert E. Lee made the statement, "It is well that war is so terrible; we should grow too fond of it."

General Burnside gathered his beaten army and headed back to Washington. Had he had the liberties to fight another way or another place it may well have been different.

With the Yankees marching home and the Army of Northern Virginia jubilant over the big victory they went into winter quarters.

This is where the great snowball fight happened. The Confederates divided, filled their heaver sacks with snowballs, and marched against each other. It was the biggest snowball foray in history.

After viewing the battle and the snowball fight Colonel Phipps was dismissed and complemented by the highest of the Confederate commanders.

General Lee, himself said, "Colonel, You have been a great service to your country, go and pillage for information that may keep the Confederacy secure."

Confederates at the wall on Marye's Heights

Chapter 9

Another Trip To The North

It did not take long on his journey north for Colonel Phipps to hear the news. Even though General Burnside's hands were tied, Lincoln fired him and on Jan 25, 1863 put in a new commander of the Army of the Potomac. This time "Fighting Joe Hooker," was the man.

General Hooker would get his army ready for a spring campaign and while he had such a huge army stationed in Washington, the whores came to town. Hooker's men had so many of the women they received the name of "Hookers" because it seemed they all belonged to Hooker's army.

Old Abe Lincoln was not done, he was sending a bigger Army this spring, and Fighting Joe Hooker was bound to capture Richmond and put an end to the South's glory.

Colonel Phipps wondered about sweet Hannah, would she still be attracted to me or will she be out of sorts about another big defeat of the Union Army?

Colonel Phipps posing as Alex the drummer had contacts in northern Virginia and all around Maryland. He had contacts with several ladies that kept an eye on Washington and the Union Army.

Alex went about and in various ways contacted Belle Boyd, Antonia Ford, Rose O'Neal Greenhow, Nancy Hart,

Laura Ratcliffe, and Loreta Janeta Velazquez. All of these ladies in one way or another supplied the south with useful information.

Hannah and Alex

Don Strivers Art

Colonel Phipps was wearing the clothes of a drummer, (peddler) yet nice. He was riding through the countryside of Maryland on this cold February and thinking about seeing Miss Hannah. He wondered how she would greet him, did she miss him, or would she be a hardheaded red head about the black eye Burnside received at Fredericksburg?

He also kept going back to the idea, should I even be with the woman that was so strong headed for the preservation of the Union. He knew he was playing with fire, yet he could not help himself. Hannah was so beautiful and so desirable. She pulled him as if a loadstone pulls a nail.

Alex would be stopping by the Adams plantation first; he really wanted to lay his eyes on the beautiful southern belle, Hannah.

As he guided Prancer toward the livery stable, he noticed the steam coming from the nostrils of Prancer. The air was so cold and his horse was so warm, it reminded Alex of a steam engine.

Just then, the black slave that tended the animals came out the barn door.

"Good moan-in Sir how is Master Alex dis fine day?" asked the Negro?" asked the Negro?

Alex smiled and threw up his hand.

"Good Morning Mister Prancer, do you mind to take care of you?" the Negro asked?

"He needs to be curried and fed, give him some water and oh! Throw a blanket on him so he don't cool down too fast," instructed Alex.

"Yes Sir Master Alex, I bee's glad to take care of that fine hoss," answered the Negro.

Alex heads to the family mansion of the Adam'. After a knock on the door, a Negro servant opens the door promptly.

The Negro smiled at Alex and said, "Come in Master Alex, get ya self outta da cold."

Alex smiled at the servant and entered the main room of the mansion. He took off his greatcoat and beaver skinned hat and handed them to the servant who gladly took them to put them away.

Oh! There she was coming through the doorway of the parlor. She had a beautiful smile on her face as she looked at him. Now Alex did not have to wonder, her beautiful smile and sparkling eyes told the whole story. The beautiful Hannah was so glad to see Alex.

Hanna skirted over to him and curtsied to him then before he knew what happened she threw her arms around him. He held her tightly, tighter than proper. They were not concerned as he pulled her breast against his chest. This was quiet a greeting and both knew the other wanted this.

Just as they released each other, William & Martha entered the room to greet Alex.

"Hello, so good to see y'all again," said Alex with that quaint southern drawl.

"How have you been Alex, have you had good sales around about?" asked Mr. Adams?

"Fine Sir, and sales have been good at several mercantile', I think the war has brought on much need for the things I sell," answered Alex.

"Well son come into the parlor and get yourself warmed and I will have some hot tea brought in, could you go for some big sugar cookies also?" Mrs. Adams asked.

"That would be so welcomed, it is quiet cold out on the roads this day," answered Alex.

Alex followed Hannah into the parlor and the house servant followed and went to the fireplace, stirred up the fire and added more wood to give them more comfort.

As soon as Hannah and Alex had sat down, a female servant arrived with a teapot full of steaming tea, two cups and a plate with several big sugar cookies.

Alex was thinking that this is great my sweet Hannah sitting with me by a warm fire and we have hot tea and cookies.

As soon as they sipped some tea, the room was left to the couple to catch up on news. It was not news they wanted just now, so Alex reached over and pulled Hannah over to his lips. She and Alex were united at the lips and the world go away for at least for this instant.

They did not have much privacy so they begin to eat cookies and sip their hot tea. They began to talk about different things. Finally, the subject of the war came to the front and it almost seemed to Alex that she was feeding him information.

Hanna stated that those dreadful rebels had tricked the great army of General Burnside and fought from behind a great stonewall. Alex listened.

Then she said, "Things will be different this spring because our great President Lincoln has put "Fighting Joe Hooker," in charge."

"Joseph Hooker is a great leader and he will be going to teach ole Bob Lee a lesson or two this spring. I heard he has a mighty big army and will meet Lee near Chancellorsville and defeat him. Then he will march on to Richmond to capture all the traitors down there."

Alex looked at Hannah and smiled, "Sweet Hannah you should not concern yourself with such matters of war or politics."

Hannah surprised Alex and called him Love, and kissed him passionately.

Hannah asked him if he would be able to stay there for the night and longer. He told her he could stay there tonight but must get out and try to get more orders from the Mercantile's in the area.

She said that she understood, but this day is short and he needed to warm and rest. You can start fresh in the morning and come back to me tomorrow night and gave him a big smile.

They sat there, held hands, drink tea, and when no one was around, they kissed. They hugged each other tightly and they both felt the love.

When no one was around they took more liberties and Hannah always held his leg. When the coast was clear, she would run her hand down inside his thigh. In addition, Alex in turn would squeeze her breast through her clothes. Oh! They had the love juices flowing.

Alex knew he was in love with Hannah and had little power to resist her. Yet she was the enemy at least a strong Union minded woman.

Now Alex knew about who would lead and where he would be coming through. As soon as possible, he would have to travel back to the Army of Northern Virginia and tell General Lee what he had learned. He wanted to talk to others to make sure the information was correct.

Two Southerners hanged for spying and treason against the United States.

Chapter 10

More Passion Than Expected

During all his travels and being stopped so many times by soldiers from both armies, Colonel Alexander Phipps was pressed into becoming a legitimate salesman ,(drummer) to the mercentile's all around Maryland.

In addition, for that period he was quite modern. He sent in his orders by telegraph and then the supplier shipped as soon as they received payment. His supplier was Connecticut Hardware Company.

Alex was contacted as to how and when the shipments were shipped. This gave him an inside line to help the Confederacy another way. When Alex knew war materials were being shipped Alex would get word to Confederate Colonel Mosby's Calvary and often the train or wagons would be taken over and the goods delivered to the Confederate Army.

Alex, (Colonel Alexander Phipps) was walking a tight rope and living on the edge; if he was caught as a spy or convicted of aiding the enemy, he would be shot or hanged.

So anytime Alex was with the beautiful Hannah it was a wonderful time of therapy for him. He could forget the world for a short time and just enjoy being with her.

This cold day after arriving at the Adams Plantation, he would spend the evening and night with Hannah and the Adams family.

After supper, Hannah and Alex sat in the parlor with Mister William and Mrs. Martha Adams and talked. In addition, they sang some songs as Hannah played the organ. Then when Hannah got tired of playing music, she got out a nice set of Ivory Dominos. They sat, played, and laughed until time for the elder Adams to retire to their feather bed.

Mrs. Martha Adams was whispering to Mister William Adams and he kept shaking his head no. She kept whispering to him and kissed his cheek and shook her head yes. Then Mister Adams shook his head yes and got up. Alex was wondering what this was all about but had an idea. Mister Adams told them good night and headed up the beautiful spiral staircase to his bedroom.

Next Mrs. Adams moved over closer to the younger couple so she could be heard. Next Mrs. Martha Adams began telling the younger couple that they are young adults and I am not going to "bundle" Alex tonight if you both promise to be prudent and behave yourself. Alex and Hannah looked at Mrs. Adams and while shaking their heads yes both said they would.

Mrs. Adams got up, turned and said, "Alright y'all stay in your own rooms and have a good night's sleep." Then she hurried up the staircase with a smile on her own face.

As soon as Mrs. Adams was up the steps and out of sight, Hannah grabbed Alex and pulled him to her with a hot kiss. They held on kissing passionately for a long time. When they both came up for air, Hannah said, "Let's Go!"

Both of their rooms were upstairs but on the opposite side of the big house from Mr. and Mrs. Adams room. They both agreed that Hannah would come to his room after the house was quiet. They both went quietly up the staircase and both smiled as they heard some giggles coming from the Adam's bedroom.

Alex would leave his door unlocked and both would go quietly to bed and wait a good hour after the house was quiet and Hannah would tip toe over to visit with Alex. Both would have their nightshirts on as a normality.

They both lay on their own featherbeds with a big quilt over them and wait. They both were thinking about what may happen.

As Hannah enters her bedroom, her mind is all-atwitter with thoughts of the handsome Alex just across the hall. She wonders if her Mother is deliberately allowing them time alone, without the restrictions of bundling. Hannah knows her parents have a very passionate love relationship. Could Mama realize how it feels to love a man and want him as much as Hannah does?

Even though Hannah had been married for a short time and was not a virgin, she was not as experienced as some might think. The time she had with William Wright was cut short so soon that she barely had time to learn to enjoy their lovemaking. However, Alex had awoken a lust within her that was unlike anything she had ever known. She knew she was falling in love with him and she wanted, more than anything, to consummate that love. Hannah had heard the servant women talk about how they pleased their man in ways other than traditional sex. She saw the excitement in them when they talked about sex with their mouths. Does she have the courage to try that with Alex?

Hannah goes to the washbasin, pours water into the bowl and splashes water onto her hot, flushed face. As she removes her dress, she notices her nipples are hard and erect against her chemise. Her pantaloons are damp with desire. She removes all her clothes and stands before the mirror with her hands cupped over her full throbbing breasts. Oh, how she wishes those were Alex's hands on her body. Hannah knows if she gives in to her desires and goes to Alex's bed there is a real possibility that she can become pregnant.

Before she knows it, the appointed hour has passed and Hannah slips into her long nightgown. She slips across the hall and slowly turns the doorknob to Alex's room.

Seeing him lying in the bed sends a flutter of desire to her nipples spiraling downward to her private area. Firelight makes shadows across his handsome face. His broad shoulders look so good and her hands itch to touch him. Hannah sees the huge bulge under the thin sheet that covers the lower half of his body. She must touch! Boldly, she walks toward the bed as Alex throws the sheet away to invite her in beside him.

Alex was so excited to see the beautiful redheaded Hannah coming to visit. She came quietly to his bed and sat beside him, they grabbed on to each other, and the kisses flowed.

When she backed off from kissing, but still real close she whispered, "You do not get everything!"

He answered, "All right," and felt of her breast through her thin nightshirt.

She in turn put her hot hand on his upper leg close to his crotch.

As they kissed, Alex ran his hand up under her nightshirt to her thigh and she put her hand on his just before it reached his goal.

Then Hannah said, "You don't get it all, keep your hand there but no further."

Alex grunted kinda disappointed.

Before Alex could be too disappointed, Hannah reached over and gripped his hard organ through his nightshirt. As she kept kissing Alex kept her hand off his organ. She raised his nightshirt, and put her hand way up his leg. Hannah found his hot hard organ, gripped it, and squeezed it in a loving way.

Alex tried to move his hand on up her leg to her hidden treasure but once again, she stopped him and said, "No you don't get it all!"

Hannah whispered to him to lay down and she pulled up his nightshirt to expose his wanting organ. She bent down over him and he could feel her hot breath on his tummy just above his hairline. Then she kissed his belly and on down on his thighs, then without any notice she kissed the head of his organ. Alex was so excited and breathing heavy now.

She still gripped his organ and without further ado, she went down on him and began to suck. Alex was about to die with excitement. His heart was pounding. He had heard of women that would do this, but actually doubted it. He thought maybe only harlots would do such a thing, but realized Hannah was a woman of good culture.

Oh! This felt so good he could hardly contain himself. They both became more aroused and she sucked hard and fast. Something had to happen soon he thought.

Then without warning, he ejaculated with his throbbing member but she hung on continuing to suck it dry. He moaned and when he could stand it no more he began to pull Hannah up. Before anything else could happen, she was kissing him on the mouth. He was thinking should I kiss her after she has done this thing. He was kinda in shock at all of this. Was there a sin or sins committed here he was thinking. Then he felt so good and relaxed he just did not care. Hannah pulled down his nightshirt, patted him on top of his head and before he could say anything she was out the door and to her own room.

Alex lay there in awe of what all had conspired. Wow, I have never had anything like this before and he felt no guilt and was so relaxed. He pulled the cover up and with a big smile on his face, he drifted off to sleep.

Next morning was about like usual, except Hannah was just a little shy, but seemed so sweet to Alex. He had his day planned and would ride away on Prancer but wanted to come back to Hannah that night if he could. Alex caught Hannah by herself to tell her bye for the day. He kissed her and whispered that she had pleased him so much and all was well. She gave him a good bear hug and he was off to the stable to get Prancer.

Alex actually went to a couple of Mercantile's, made some sales, and then headed to the Wellington's Plantation to see John Wellington.

Alex, (Colonel Alexander Phipps), had important information to give to General Lee. Sure enough, Ole Lincoln had made Fighting Joe Hooker the commander of the Army of the Potomac and he would waste little time heading south. Alex must ride straight to the Army of Northern Virginia. Thank goodness, he would ride by the Adams Plantation and he would be able to give Hannah a proper hug and goodbye.

Alex talked to Prancer as they traveled toward the Adams Plantation. Prancer moved his ears around as if he understood every word. Alex told him it looks like he is in trouble and that he was in love with a Yankee Loving Woman. Prancer whinnied in protest and Alex laughed aloud.

Alex made it to the Adams Plantation, gave the stable man orders to leave the saddle on Prancer but water him. Please give him some oats, as they would be traveling more on that cold evening.

As the stable man went about his business Alex went straight to the house and as soon as the door was opened to him he went straight way to the parlor.

Hannah met him and helped him take off his great coat. She took him over by the fireplace to warm while they talked. He told her he had to travel on and would be back as soon as possible. It may be spring, but I will come back to you.

Alex whispered for the first time, "Hannah, I Love You!"

"Awww, Alex I am so glad, I too am in love with you," she said.

He held her tight looked into her eyes and gave her a passionate kiss, picked up his great coat and put it on. Hannah buttoned him in as warm as she could and he left her with big tears running down her face.

Colonel Phipps made it through the lines that night and was to General Lee himself late the next night.

General Lee would gather his winter army of a meager 60,000 and face Hooker with 131,000 man Army.

Chapter 11

Hooker Comes Calling

General Lee and his officers are concerned that Lincoln and Joseph Hooker has had four months to put together a great army of 131,000 men. In addition, General Hooker is known to be aggressive and will come to crush the Army of Northern Virginia and end the war.

During the winter, many of Lee's men went home and some are slow to get back as they plow the fields for the summer crops. When all was said and done General Lee will be at Chancellorsville with his small, but determined army of 60,892 men.

The Hooker Army had around 400 cannon to around 200 for the Lee army.

If anything General Hooker's army had much confidence this time. General Lee hoped they had too much confidence and maybe think an easy victory would be theirs.

There was much praying in the south as they learned of the unsurmountable odds that was against them. Thinking God was with them as HE was with David when he faced the giant Goliath with only a sling shot, but gave the boy David the victory, the south marched with faith.

General Hooker came calling and even had a good-sized army to cross at Fredericksburg to circle around behind the Southern army.

Colonel Alexander Phipps was with Lee as he watched this all unfold. What would the Wiley Old Gray Fox, (Robert E. Lee) do this time to out General Joe Hooker?

The largest army to face the Confederacy to date was the Union Army and it crossed the Rappahannock River on April 27, 1863. They concentrated near Chancellorsville, Virginia on April 30, 1863.

Fighting Joe Hooker

General Stonewall Jackson

General Robert E. Lee

General Lee and his top officers met on the evening of April 30 and while they met Calvary General J.E.B. Stuart rode into camp with scouting report.

J.E.B. Stuart

The report had a big bearing on what General Lee would do. Also General Stonewall Jackson made a recommedation that would act on the scouting report.

General Hookers left flank was so at ease and unprepared it was determined that would be at the place to strike in a surprise flanking move and General Lee would send General Jackson's whole corps. This would divided the small Southern Army and Lee also sent 11,000 to defend at Fredericksburg under General

Jubal Earley to defend against Union Union General Sedgwick's 40,000 man army. The Confederates held against two asaults then the Union army flew the flag of truce to gather the dead and wonded. While they were doing that they saw up close the very few men they were fightning. Then they launched another attack and pushed back the Southerns.

Later with this small army Jubal Early would surround Sedgwick's army on three sides and drive them back across the river.

With what Army that was left, Lee would hold the center. This kind of maneuvering was unheard of. A small Army being divided in the presence of a much more powerful army.

General Hooker had on his right flank the XI corps that were to be used as reserves. That day it was getting to be supper time and the XI Corps was at ease cooking and goofing off.

Stonewall Jackson had marched his men quietly all day and was ready to pounce. At about 5:30 21,500 men came rushing out of the woods screaming the "Rebel Yell" and threw the Union XI Corps into panic.

By 7:30 Jackson's Second Corps, had advanced to within a quarter mile of Chancellorsville. Now darkness was closing in and both armies were confused and General Jackson wanted to push on. He Junior officers talked him out of it saying "Sir, We don't know who we may be fighting our men are scaztterd all around." Jackson would not be still, he had to go and spy on the Yankee Army to form a plan for the next morning. Tradegy struck as he and his officers came up on some of the Confederate infantry, and were mistaken for Yankee Calvary. A hale of bullets were fired at Jackson and his officers. One stuck Jackson in the left arm and shattered the bone. They got him to safety but the arm had to be amputated. Jackson should have lived but came down with pneumonia and died a few days later. J.E.B. Stuart took over the Confederate second Corps and with heavy fighting from them and General Lee's men. Hooker lost his nerve and withdrew.

My plans are perfect. May God have mercy on General Lee for I will have none.

Maj. Gen. Joseph Hooker

Summery of the Battle

The **Battle of Chancellorsville** was a major battle of the American Civil War, and the principal engagement of the **Chancellorsville Campaign**. It was fought from April 30 to May 6, 1863, in Spotsylvania County, Virginia, near the village of Chancellorsville. Two related battles were fought nearby on May 3 near Fredericksburg. The campaign pitted Union Army Maj. Gen. Joseph Hooker's Army of the Potomac against an army less than half its size, Gen. Robert E. Lee's Confederate Army of Northern Virginia. Chancellorsville is known as Lee's "perfect battle" because his risky decision to divide his army in the presence of a much larger enemy force resulted in a significant Confederate victory. The victory, a product of Lee's audacity and Hooker's timid decision making, was tempered by heavy casualties and the mortal wounding of Lt. Gen. Thomas J. "Stonewall" Jackson to friendly fire, a loss that Lee likened to "losing my right arm."

The Chancellorsville Campaign began with the crossing of the Rappahannock River by the Union army on the morning of April 27, 1863. Union Calvary under Maj. Gen. George Stoneman began a long distance raid against Lee's supply lines at about the same time. This operation was completely ineffectual. Crossing the Rapidan River via Germanna and Ely's Fords, the Federal infantry concentrated near Chancellorsville on April 30. Combined with the Union force facing Fredericksburg, Hooker planned a double envelopment, attacking Lee from both his front and rear.

On May 1, Hooker advanced from Chancellorsville toward Lee, but the Confederate general split his army in the face of superior numbers, leaving a small force at Fredericksburg to deter Maj. Gen. John Sedgwick from advancing, while he attacked Hooker's advance with about 4/5 of his army. Despite the objections of his subordinates, Hooker withdrew his men to the defensive lines around Chancellorsville, ceding the initiative to Lee. On May 2, Lee divided his army again, sending Stonewall Jackson's entire corps on a flanking march that routed the Union XI Corps. While performing a personal reconnaissance in advance of his line, Jackson was wounded by fire from his own men, and Maj. Gen. J.E.B. Stuart temporarily replaced him as corps commander. The fiercest fighting of the battle; and the second bloodiest day of the Civil War; occurred on May 3 as Lee launched multiple attacks against the Union position at Chancellorsville, resulting in heavy losses on both sides. That same day, Sedgwick advanced across the Rappahannock River, defeated the small Confederate force at Marye's Heights in the Second Battle of Fredericksburg and then moved to the west. The Confederates fought a successful delaying action at the Battle of Salem Church and by May 4 had driven back Sedgwick's men to Banks's Ford, surrounding them on three sides. Sedgwick withdrew across the ford early on May 5, and Hooker withdrew the remainder of his army across U.S. Ford the night of May 5–6. The campaign ended on May 7 when Stoneman's Calvary reached Union lines east of Richmond.

Hailed the presence of a victorious chief. He sat in the full realization of all that soldiers' dream of—triumph; and as I looked at him in the complete fruition of the success which his genius, courage, and confidence in his army had won, I thought that it must have been from some such scene that men in ancient days ascended to the dignity of gods.

Charles Marshall, Lee's military secretary, An Aide-de-Camp to Lee

My God! It is horrible—horrible; and to think of it, 130,000 magnificent soldiers so cut to pieces by less than 60,000 half-starved rag muffins!

Horace Greeley, New York Tribune

My God! My God! What will the people say?

Abraham Lincoln

Chapter 12

Colonel Phipps Hurries North

General Lee and all the South laments over the loss of their beloved Stonewall Jackson. General Lee would not go and visit General Jackson, he said he would rather meet him when he returned to duty. General Lee could not fathom that General Jackson is dieing. But the loss of an arm did not kill him he died from pneumonia.

General Jackson was one of the most devout Christians in his time. He prayed often and quoted his Bible as well. He believed that God was with him in all things and was not afraid in battle.

Near the end of his life with friends and family gathered about him he was shouting out orders as in battle, then he got quiet and said, *"Let us cross over the river and rest under the shade of the trees!"*

After General Lee had received recmmemdations from President Jefferson Davis to send men to the Western part of the war because the south was loosing to the stronger Union attacks. General Lee had another idea, he would take a strong army and invade the north. This would serve three purposes, one to pull back the Union pressure in the west and also let Lee's army replensih from the breadbasket of the north. And the main thing Lee was thinking was that if he could draw out the Union Army and defeat it the war would be over. After all his smaller but inspired army had just won the last two battles against great odds.

The summer of 1863 General Lee could muster a 75,000 man army.

Alex is back in his drummer clothes and is riding Prancer all around Maryland, getting orders and keeping his ear to the ground. He is so anxious to get back to the William Adams Plantation. But he hears much talk about just letting the South be and forget all the killing. People were even talking about the election next time. Some said they would not vote for a pro-war candidate. Some of the comments were how the rag-tag rebel army kept whipping the bigger stronger and better equiped Army of the Potomac. Alex thought, these people are getting tired of the war, maybe one more victory will turn the tide.

Alex was getting all the orders he could and gathering all the information he could, but it was time to go and see his beautiful Hannah. He was hoping that nothing would come up and he could spend several days with the Adams family.

The Yankees were stilling reeling from the whipping they took at Chancellorsville and were not apt to come charging back south for some time.

It was spring time and all of the birds and bees were busy planning on multiplying their kind. Funny thing, in spring all of God's critters seek out a mate and even mankind.

Alex was enjoying the weather and had that gorgeous redheaded Hannah on his mind. This trip he was hoping to spend more time with Hannah. Nothing seems to be too pressing this time as Alex comes to see Hannah. The North is not likely to come back to Virginia in the near future as they are still reeling from Chancellorsville. Alex could relax have some fun and be with Hannah, except he needed to check about for information and keep his ear to the ground.

It was a beautiful early June day when Alex rode in to the Adams Plantation. The place was a bussel with folks out working in the fields and even in the flower gardens. The Adams ladies were explaining to the Negroes how to plant the flowers so the garden would be beautiful when they were all in bloom.

As Alex approched on his fine horse, Prancer, Hannah looked up ran to him. She grabbed the reigns and stopped Prancer. Alex bounded from the saddle and grabbed Hannah and picked her up off the ground. Holding her tight he spun her around with her feet never touching the ground. He sat her down and she burst into tears of happiness. Oh what a reunion for the young couple.

Martha and the excited Negroes stood in awe and enjoyed the reunion of the two lovebirds.

One of the Negro Ladies spoke up before she realized it, "Dat Miss Hannah suh loves dat Mister Alex!"

Martha turned and looked at her and gave her a little curt smile. Then the servant girl turned back quickly to face her chores.

Alex and Hannah walked hand in hand to the stable leading Prancer. After Alex knew his fine horse would be cared for he walked Lady Hannah back to the big house.

Hannah told Alex, "You are not going to run off so quick this time, are you?"

Alex smiled at her and said, "Hope not, I think I can stay a few days."

Hannah then said, "Good, we can go on picnics and buggy rides, and even go to town together."

After Alex took his saddle bags and carpet bag in the house and sat them down, Hannah took him by the hand and led him to the gazebo. A servant girl asked Miss Hannah if they wanted tea brought to them?

Hannah asked her to bring some tea and maybe a fresh cookie for both of them.

"Yes Miss Hannah, I bees right back in a jest a bit," answered the servant girl.

After Hannah and Alex had sat down and exchanges a kiss or two, the tea was brought and poured into fine china cups with matching saucers. Hannah dismissed the servant with a smile and more kisses were exchanged.

They kissed in between sups of tea and would stop and hold each other tightly. Hannah would grip the upper part of Alex' leg and he put his hand on her breast. Oh what a hot couple they were.

With a little talking here and there, Hannah would look to see if anyone could see them, then she would actually put her hand in his crotch and his member was aleady hard. His pants had the love bulge and Hannah would give him a sweet little grin. Time flew as the love birds sat, talked and courted. Then Hannah saw the servant girl coming to tell them it was supper time.

After supper William and Martha Adams asked Alex and Hannah to join then on the porch for a brandy and a cigar. Of course the ladies did not take the cigars or brandy, only the conversation. Actually many ladies of the time smoked pipes or even chewed tobacco.

They had pleasant conversations at first, then the subject came up about the war. Alex was surprised at what William and Martha were saying. They were speaking of the last two battles in which the Army of the Potomack were sent back north with a black eye.

William said, "I think it is time for the north to let the South be and let them have their own country. We are wasting so many precious lifes in this needless war."

Martha even gave her opinion as women did in private conversations with family.

Martha said, "Just let Lee and his Army alone, we can't seem to beat them, if we keep this up I fear Lee will bring his army to to the north."

Martha was refering to the last two battles, Fredericksburg and Chancellorsville when she said we can't beat them anyway even with twice the number of men.

Hannah sit quietly but kept smiling at her Alex.

Alex was thinking, wonder if most of the northern people share these sentments about the war. If General Lee wins one more big battle, or Lincoln is voted out the South will be free from the North.

As darkness fell on the Adams Plantation William and Martha got up and went into the house. All the windows were raised to about six inches but were blocked from going any higher for security reasons. The slaves on this plantation had never shown any aggression but in the deep south some had uprisings. It was just good sense to be prudent.

It was a custom to go to bed early and rise early out on the plantations, so as Martha went in she turned to Hannah and said, "Honey, you and Mister Phipps better come in shortly and please bolt the door."

"Yes Momma, we will be right in," answered Hannah.

After a couple more kisses Alex and Hannah joined the elder Adams' in the parlor for a night-cap.

The four sat and talked for a little while and William stood and said, "Good night to you folks I am retiring."

Then he said a little saying, "To bed to bed, said sleeply head!"

"Oh no said slow!"

"Put on the pot said greedy gut and we will eat before we go!"

All of them laughed, and Alex said, "Tell greedy gut to go to bed I am not ready to eat again."

They all smiled and William headed up the spirral staircase to bed.

Martha stood and gave the young couple walking orders, "no bundling, but I expect both of you to behave and stay in your own rooms!"

"Yes Momma, you have a good nights sleep, we will retire soon." Said Hannah.

Alex and Hannah had a great feeling about each other it was not just lust, but it had turned into a pure love.

Chapter 13

Hot Summer Night

Alex and Hannah were alone for a great kiss before heading up the spiral staircase to their rooms. They stood and held on to each other so tight. Hannah whispered for the first time, "Mister Alexander Phipps I love you."

Alex caught a new breath of air and exhaled, "My Hannah I love you, come to my room later please."

"Yes Darling just as soon as my parents are asleep, I will be there," answered Hannah in a sweet whisper.

The two held hands going up the long flight of stairs squeezed hands and went toward their own rooms. Alex stopped and moved his mouth and uttered the words, "Hannah, I have missed you and I want you."

Hannah smiled at him and turned into her bedroom.

Martha Adams cracked open her door for a quick look to see if Hannah was going to her room. She closed the door and went to William who was waiting with his arms open for his wife. She got in bed, snuggled up close, and whispered, "All is alright, and the children are in their own rooms."

After about an hour had passed and the house was quiet, then Hannah tiptoed to Alex's room. He was sitting on the bed with his oil lamp burning. He looked up and smiled. Hannah walked over and sit beside him and they kissed. Then she said, "Alex where do you go and why do you stay gone so long from me?"

Alex was not expecting a direct question this time of night. He looked into her expecting eyes and said, "In time my love, I will tell you all about my travels and where I go, but for now just trust me."

Hannah looked back at Alex kinda disappointed in his answer. Then she stated that she noticed he was always away when the armies had their big battles and come back soon as they were over.

"I think I know what you do but will not press for an answer now, but if you truly love me you will have to tell me all. We cannot have secrets from each other.

Alex looked at her as if she was a little girl and said, "For now my love, trust me and in due time you will know all. You do know I am a drummer and this takes me all over the state."

"Yes, I know, but there is more to it, think about it I have to know soon if our relationship can grow." She answered.

Now things were calm and Hannah was at peace with the answer Alex gave. They sat on the bed and kissed.

Alex soon had his hand on her breast. Then both breast. Then he gently pulled up her nightshirt and she raised her arms so he could lift it over her head. There she sat in the dim light with her young firm breast protruding like two beautiful hungry fawns.

Alex held her beautiful breast and soon started kissing them. He would gently pinch her nipples and take turns sucking first one then the other.

Hannah whispered, "You don't get it all tonight, just my breasts for now."

Alex did not answer but kept sucking her now hard protruding nipples and she moaned with pleasure.

Hannah could not contain herself so she reached down and found his bulging hard member. She gently unbuttoned his pants and let his stiffness expand out of the opening.

"Alex I so want all of you, but not now, too many question not answered," she said.

Alex was so busy loving on her breast that he gave her a little moan for an answer and kept sucking her breasts.

They both were thinking and wondering, what do I really know about the other person? They were so aroused that they kept at it. She gripped his hard member and he sucked her breasts, and then he tried to run his hand up her dress. She put a strong hand on his before he could fine her treasure.

"No Alex you cannot have it all, not now," she whispered.

Hannah pushed Alex back gently and laid him down on the bed. Then she stood up and pulled his pants and drawers off. Then she sat back down on the edge of the bed.

Then it happened Hannah leaned over and started kissing him all around his stiff organ and even kissed his sack of balls. Alex was so aroused that Hannah marveled at the hardness she had helped create.

While she playfully went about his member, Alex found her breast again and held them by their nipples. Hannah could not hold back she took his hard member into her mouth and sucked. She went up and down on it almost swallowing it on the downward plunges. Alex legs stiffened as she had her way with his organ.

Finally, his toes curled and hid member throbbed and ejaculated, but Hannah kept it up until Alex could take it no more. She loved to please her man and she had finished him to the last drop of his shooting semen. Alex lay there like a dead man for about a minute and then she lay beside him and they kissed deeply.

Alex was worried about Hannah. She needs the same kind of relief so he reversed his position and started blowing hot air on Hannah's forbidden treasure. Before long, he had pulled up her nightshirt and had his face close to her hot crack. He kissed between her thighs and on both sides then he kissed her sweet lips between the hairs. Next, he took his tongue and licked her crack. Before long, his tongue penetrated into the hot juicy mouth of her womanhood. She spread her long beautiful legs more and she pulled his head to her crotch. His tongue tickled all over her hardened clitoris and she moaned out loud. She quickened and hunched on his mouth and tongue and had several orgasms. Then she exploded with a great orgasm. Now she lay motionlessly for a few minutes.

Hannah could not ever remember such lovemaking and such power of release. She changed direction, took Alex's face in her hands, and kissed him deeply.

Hannah then rose up quickly, gave one last kiss for the night, and tiptoed to her room. All was quiet and both were well satisfied in a most wonderful way. They both marveled at the night's experience but were so relaxed they fell off to a wonderful slumber.

The next day all was fine. Nothing was said between the two lovers other than normal chitchat.

Alex had standing orders to discover any enemy movements and information. To do this he would take daylong trips to take orders as a drummer and listen to what folks said. Then of course, he had certain contacts that were always gathering information and relaying it to him.

There were no new threats coming out of Washington so Alex was take more time in Maryland to be close to Hannah.

This new day was pretty and most comfortable so Hannah ask Alex to take her to town to do some shopping. They borrowed the Adams Family buggy and headed into Hagerstown.

This trip they were more settled and talked about lots of things as they enjoyed the early summer scenery.

Alex drove the buggy up in front of the main stores, got off the buggy and tied the horse to a hitching post then walked back to help Hannah down from the buggy . As Hannah stepped down on the board sidewalk, she glanced up and saw her Cousin Ginger approaching with a big smile and with her fan over her face.

With Permission of Gloria Nikki Bell

Rendition of Ginger

Chapter 14
Ginger

"Henrietta, you are a sight for sore eyes, who may I as is this handsome gentleman escorting you about?" asked Gloria?

Hannah gave Ginger a little hug and said, "You look bodacious as usual.

Ginger looked back with a little competiveness showing. "This is Alexander Phipps, he is a drummer and is staying at my house," said Hannah very passively.

"Oh! Cousin Henrietta, I do not intend to steal your handsome feller," answered Ginger.

Alex is standing there in awe, looking at the two most beautiful ladies in all the country, North and South.

Ginger covered her mouth with her fan winked her eye, curtsied, and presented her dainty gloved hand to Alex. Alex took her hand, bowed, and kissed her hand. Electricity flowed.

Alex was overcome and thought how beautiful Ginger was and knew that she knew she was beautiful and a flirt.

"Well Cousin Ginger come see me, ya hear, Alex and I have shopping to do," said Hannah. It was obvious Hannah wanted to get Alex away from the beautiful Ginger.

"Well y'all scoodle-do and have fun." Said Ginger with a wink from her beautiful blue eye.

"Oh! Did y'all hear about the ball on Saturday night at the town hall?" asked Ginger before Hannah could pull Alex away.
"No we have not heard, will it be grand?" asked Hannah?
"Yes it will be grand, if you bring that handsome Alexander, I will save him a dance," answered Ginger with a big smile.

Alex actually blushed, but gave Ginger a big smile. Hannah took his hand and starting dragging him down the plank sidewalk and their shoes sounded like a horse trotting. Hannah knew her cousin and she would steal Alex in a heartbeat if she could.

Alex was thinking how beautiful Ginger was and knew she did not hold back with her flirting. He wondered if there was something in the water around Hagerstown that produced two beautiful red heads. He wondered if Ginger would be a Hellcat in bed, or if she was just a big tease.
He turned his thoughts to the woman that held his hand, and then he thought there is none finer than this woman Hannah.

I think the cousins were just butting heads in competition he concluded.

Hannah was kinda quiet while they shopped and then on the way back home, she begin to ask questions.

"Alex, what do you see in our future?"

"Alex, what is your real purpose?"
I know you come to me then in a short time you rush off. You always go just before a big battle and then you come back after the battle is over.

"You and I are so much like our country, we stay divided, and then back you come, please tell me what is going on," said Hannah.

Alex listened intently, and then said, "My beautiful Hannah, if I tell you all I am so afraid I will lose you." However, I will tell you this, "I love you and will not hurt you, I have things that I have sworn to protect, and in time I will tell you all. Please respect my wishes and just love me!"

The week went on with love sessions every night but no penetration. Saturday night came and Hannah, Alex, William, and Martha would all ride the family carriage with their well-trained black driver. Hannah and Alex sit dignified in the family Carriage and carried on with pleasant conversation. The evening was very festive, but Hannah expected her opposition, Ginger to try to capture Alex at the ball.

The town hall was decorated with red, white, and blue banners and many Maryland and United States flags. The town hall had a spacious room for big gatherings and of course town balls. There was a large table set up with fancy tablecloth, all kinds of delicous little treats, a couple of punch bowls full of punch (most likely spiked) and some fine wine. In addition, there were a box of cigars. It was all lit up with candles and much color. The building was lit up with hundreds of oil lamps and candles.

Chairs were placed all around the walls except one end; there were several nice tables and chairs there for the VIP's of Hagerstown.

After Hannah, Alex, Martha, and William made it through the gauntlet of greeters and friends the younger couple found a seat by the wall.
There she was the ravishing redheaded Ginger and she sashayed over towards Hannah and Alex. Hannah smiled but her claws were coming out. If Cousin Ginger released her flirtation on Alex there may be a pussycat fight.

Two gentlemen had followed after Ginger to ask her for a dance or whatever. Ginger attracted the men like flies on a dead skunk. Ginger turned to them and said, "Hold it boys I will give you both a dance tonight, but I need to be with my sweet cousin Henrietta right now. Both men bowed and walked away and Ginger gave them that smile that would make a grown man lay down and beg. "Hello my sweet Henrietta and you my handsome Alex," said Ginger.

She held her fan to hide most of her face but her eyes spoke volumes to Alex.

Alex stood, bowed, and took her hand and kissed it; Ginger curtsied and pretended to blush.
Hannah was thinking that Ginger would not blush in a whorehouse.

Then Hannah rose, and gave her cousin a little hug, but her face was red with growing rage.

Ginger smiles at Hannah and said, Sweet Cousin, I am sure you do not mind me taking Alex for a dance, I see the Grand March is about to start.
"Of course not," said Hannah in a sarcastic manner.

There they went, Alex in tow for the Grand March.
Damn that redheaded bitch, here five minutes and she has him for the Grand March, thought Hannah.

Hannah sit there watching the Grand March and Alex was being led around the dance hall. They were going arm in arm and hand in hand. They were both smiling.

Ginger was squeezing his hand in a very seductive way and Alex squeezed back. The electricity was flowing and they looked at each other as often as they could.

Ginger told Alex to watch for a chance to be with her, she told him she might get a headache and have to leave, she would need an escort to take her home. Alex was not sure of all of this, he felt as if he was in the middle and actually cheating on Hannah, but he never said anything. Alex was drawn to this redheaded Ginger and she was doing the drawing.

The Grand March was over, and Alex bowed to Ginger and said, "I must get back to Hannah."

As soon as he was back with Hannah, he asked her to dance and they were on the floor until their faces were red and needed to sit some out.

As the evening was going well and Hannah and Alex cooled off drinking punch and talking, here come Ginger again. Ginger came to them and then touching both on their shoulders and then looked to be in terrible pain.

Hannah thought something may be awry, but asked Ginger what was wrong.

Ginger gave them a pitiful look and said, "I have a sick headache, Alex would you be a dear and escort me home?

"Why can't your escort that brought you here take you home?" asked Hannah?

In a quiet pitiful voice Ginger whispered, "My father Archibald Adams brought me. He was going to send a carriage to carry me home at about 11 O'clock because he felt ill also." " I am afraid I can't wait that long, Alex please take me home," she persisted.

Hannah looked forlorn but said, "Alex you ought to carry her home, but please get back soon."

Hannah whispered to him, "You better behave!"

Poor Alex was stuck in the middle of a feud between two beautiful redheads. It was scary but also fun he thought.

Alex walked slowly with Ginger on his arm and she led him to her buggy. He helped her up into the buggy and then untied the horse and climbed into the seat with Ginger. Ginger wasted no time getting close to him and as soon as the horse had them on the road, she took her hand and turned his head toward her giving him a hot seductive kiss.

As they kissed, Ginger squeezed his leg and then moved her hand to his crotch and his member was rising with excitement.

Alex looked down the road a time or two to see where they were going, but knew the horse knew the way home.

They were kissing more and more and before Alex knew it, Ginger had his pants unbuttoned and his member in her grip. She jacked it a time or two while they kissed then without notice she bent over and had him in her hot mouth.

Alex was so aroused, by now his legs stiffened and he moaned. Suddenly his exploding ejaculation filled her mouth with semen but she never wavered from the throbbing. She kept it up until he was practically begging her to stop. She rose up, grabbed him, and gave him a long hot juicy kiss.

Alex stopped the buggy to catch his breath and Ginger had his hand under her hoops. She pushed his hand up her leg into her crotch less pantaloons right into her treasure. Alex felt her wetness and worked two fingers between her lips and into her vaginal pleasure. Ginger spread wide as he begin to finger against her clitoris and she was screaming with pleasure. It never took long she has a big orgasm and relaxed back against the buggy seat.

Ginger panted and turned to Alex for another hot kiss. Then she said, "Damn Alex I sure needed that, wish I could take him inside me but better not."

Alex got the horse moving again and soon they were at her the Archibald Adams home.

Ginger looked at Alex and said, "You handsome man, funny my headache is gone, drive me back to the ball."

Alex had enjoyed it all but was perturbed at her also. He hoped this would not mess him up with Hannah; He loved Hannah even though he had cheated on her.

They got back to the ball in time for a few more dances and Hannah was glad to have her man back. Ginger stayed away for the rest of the evening.

Chapter 15

Lee's Determined Army Goes North

General Lee was going to have to make a decision, send a large portion of his army to help in the western part of the war, or invade the North to draw the enemy troops away from the west and maybe defeat the Union in one big battle. He decided, after his men had always accomplished what he has set before them, he would head north.

Messengers riding and telegraph lines were humming with the news, "The Whole Damn Rebel Army was heading north."

It was mostly true that General Lee had gathered a huge number of veteran soldiers and did not leave too many behind.

This time Lee skirted through the gaps into the Shenandoah Valley and headed to Pennsylvania. However, early on the folks in the north were so alarmed, which way will they come?

The Northern News Papers had painted a black picture of the Army of Northern Virginia; they were thought to be rapist, thieves, and all that could be bad. They did not know the honorable Confederate soldiers. Yes, they would procure foods and supplies, livestock and anything the army had need of, but all would paid with money of the Confederates States of America.

Some of the towns and merchants committed that at least the south paid, even with worthless money, but the North took as they wanted and often did not pay.

With all this news, Alex would have to leave again so he went to Hannah and told her he has important business he had to attend to and must leave.

Hannah was in tears as her emotions were running high and now Alex would leave her with the Rebels coming.

"Alex, what is so important that you have to leave me in this crisis?" asked Hannah?

"You will be just fine, they will not bother you," exclaimed Alex.

"Just how do you know this and where are you going, my love?" asked Hannah?

"They are not the cutthroat molesters that Northern Folks make them out to be," said Alex.

The Newspapers are full of lies and cause so much mistrust. They want the North to hate the southern people because they want to keep them for the tax money and cotton," said Alex.

"It is time you tell me what you are and what you do," demanded Hannah.

Alex held her and looked into her beautiful eyes, and whispered softly, "Hannah my love, I hope to tell you everything when I return."

"Even if the truth divides us," he continued.

"End of us? What do you mean my love?" Asked Hannah.

"I so hope it will never end us, but I am not sure you will be able to stand what I will say at that time," answered Alex.

"Hannah my Darling let it go for now and just stay in love with me," pleaded Alex.

"I will my love I promise, come back to me safe and sound," answered Hannah.

Alex gathered his gear and his mysterious carpetbag and went to get Prancer, with Hannah holding his arm all the way.

The stable man had saddled Prancer already. Alex mounted and rode out about twenty yards and wheeled

Prancer around. Then the two lovers, waved and Colonel Alexander Phipps headed south.

Colonel Phipps had news that Hooker was coming after General Lee, but in the process, General George Mead had been placed in command of the Northern Army replacing General Hooker. Also the news that the whole north was scared to death of the Confederate army.

As soon as Colonel Phipps was a few miles from Hagerstown, he stopped and changed into his Confederate Uniform even though it could be risky. That was what had been in the carpetbag all this time.

Colonel Phipps hoped to be on the staff of General Lee, but he would take command of a unit if asked.

Two days riding and being chased by some Union Calvary the Colonel met up with the point guard of the Confederate Army.

After being checked by the men in front they sent him back down the long line of gray and butternut clad soldiers. They were ragged and dirty and many had no shoes, but you could see in their eyes the determination to win their freedom. Discipline was lacking except in a fight, so many of the soldiers waved and hollered at the Colonel as he passed.

Colonel Phipps was so impressed with such a magnificent Army. The numbers and the Spirit he saw. Yet he realized that some 20,000 men would outnumber this army.

Colonel Phipps passed many cannon and wagons as he headed down the line. Finally, Colonel Phipps was told that General Lee was riding Traveler a short way back. When he saw the General, he was surrounded with several staff offices.

General Lee was a gentleman and mostly a quiet spoken commander, but all admired him.

All through Maryland, West Virginia, and Pennsylvania were getting ready. They were boarding up buildings trying to hide valuables and even themselves.

Hannah and Martha Adams and most women were given guns for self-defense. They all had refresher courses as how to shoot but were told not to provoke the Southern men if they came around.

Colonel Alexander Phipps was joined to General Lee's staff and would serve as a courier between headquarters and the corps commanders.

The Old Gray Fox, (General Lee) had a smile appear on his face when he was told that General George Mead had replaced General Joe Hooker. Mead would be the fifth Union Commander that Lee and his rag-tag army would face.

The great Southern Army marched towards Pennsylvania and bypassed Hagerstown Maryland. Lee was restocking his army from the fat of the North. One thing he hoped to find was shoes for his men as so many of his men marched barefoot. He also wanted to have one last battle, defeat the Union Army, and then demand that the Confederate States of America be recognized as a free and independent nation.

The corn was up in the fields and many of the Confederates ate the green corn, which caused mass diarrhea. Many a time the soldiers would leave the march and run to the bushes. The word was passed down the line not to eat the green corn. Soon the foragers started bringing in good food and meat and the men once again enjoyed good eating. The foragers rounded up, horses, cattle, and all edible farm animals. They also picked up anything that would help the army. It was not taken outright as the Union Army often did, as they called confiscated. At least the Confederates paid for what they took. They paid in Confederate Money.

General Lee felt good about his campaign because his army had always performed just as he had asked. This time 20,000 men would only outnumber his army.

Hannah and Ginger were in the same boat so to speak. They were both afraid of the Confederates that were going about the countryside foraging for food and supplies. Archibald had brought his family over to the William Adams plantation for safety. This put Hannah and Cousin Ginger together and there were no competition because the good-looking Alex Phipps was gone. They talked about lots of things including the good times of growing up together, but never was a word spoken about Ginger having Alex drive her home and then back to the ball. Ginger even felt bad about her behavior that night. Hannah suspected that Ginger made advances to Alex but let it go and gave Ginger the benefit of a doubt

Orders were given to all even the slaves to cooperate with the soldiers if they came by. Lots of the valuables and other things were hidden if they could be. The southern men were not to be provoked, but if things got dangerous, shoot to kill.

Hannah missed Alex so bad and she worried that he was not telling her everything. She had fallen in love with Alex and wanted more than a relationship; she wanted to be married to him.

Chapter 16

Gettysburg Campaign

The Battle of Gettysburg was fought July 1–3, 1863, in and around the town of Gettysburg, Pennsylvania between Union and Confederate forces during the American Civil War. The battle involved the largest number of casualties of the entire war and is often described as the war's turning point. Union Maj. Gen. George Meade's Army of the Potomac defeated attacks by Confederate Gen. Robert E. Lee's Army of Northern Virginia, ending Lee's invasion of the North.

After his success at Chancellorsville in Virginia in May 1863, Lee led his army through the Shenandoah Valley to begin his second invasion of the North—the Gettysburg Campaign. With his army in high spirits, Lee intended to shift the focus of the summer campaign from war-ravaged northern Virginia and hoped to influence Northern politicians to give up their prosecution of the war by penetrating as far as Harrisburg, Pennsylvania, or even Philadelphia. Prodded by President Abraham Lincoln, Maj. Gen. Joseph Hooker moved his army in pursuit, but was relieved just three days before the battle and replaced by Meade.

Elements of the two armies initially collided at Gettysburg on July 1, 1863, as Lee urgently concentrated his forces there, his objective being to engage the Union army and destroy it. Low ridges to the northwest of town were defended initially by a Union cavalry division under Brig. Gen. John Buford, and soon reinforced with two corps of Union infantry. However, two large Confederate corps assaulted them from the northwest and north, collapsing the hastily developed Union lines, sending the defenders retreating through the streets of town to the hills just to the south.

On the second day of battle, most of both armies had assembled. The Union line was laid out in a defensive formation resembling a fishhook. In the late afternoon of July 2, Lee launched a heavy assault on the Union left flank, and fierce fighting raged at Little Round Top, the Wheatfield, Devil's Den, and the Peach Orchard. On the Union right, Confederate demonstrations escalated into full-scale assaults on Culp's Hill and Cemetery Hill. All across the battlefield, despite significant losses, the Union defenders held their lines.

On the third day of battle, July 3, fighting resumed on Culp's Hill, and cavalry battles raged to the east and south, but the main event was a dramatic infantry assault by 12,500 Confederates against the center of the Union line on Cemetery Ridge, known as Pickett's Charge. The charge was repulsed by Union rifle and artillery fire, at great losses to the Confederate army.

Lee led his army on a torturous retreat back to Virginia. Between 46,000 and 51,000 soldiers from both armies were casualties in the three-day battle.

On November 19, President Lincoln used the dedication ceremony for the Gettysburg National Cemetery to honor the fallen Union soldiers and redefine the purpose of the war in his historic Gettysburg Address.

Shortly after the Army of Northern Virginia won a major victory over the Army of the Potomac at the Battle of Chancellorsville (April 30 – May 6, 1863), Robert E. Lee decided upon a second invasion of the North (the first was the unsuccessful Maryland Campaign of September 1862, which ended in the bloody Battle of Antietam). Such a move would upset Federal plans for the summer campaigning season and possibly reduce the pressure on the besieged Confederate garrison at Vicksburg. The invasion would allow the Confederates to live off the bounty of the rich Northern farms while giving war-ravaged Virginia a much-needed rest. In addition, Lee's 72,000-man army could threaten Philadelphia, Baltimore, and Washington, and possibly strengthen the growing peace movement in the North.

Thus, on June 3, Lee's army began to shift northward from Fredericksburg, Virginia. Following the death of Thomas J. "Stonewall" Jackson, Lee reorganized his two large corps into three new corps, commanded by Lt. Gen. James Longstreet (First Corps), Lt. Gen. Richard S.

Ewell (Second), and Lt. Gen. A.P. Hill (Third); both Ewell and Hill, who had formerly reported to Jackson as division commanders, were new to this level of responsibility. The Cavalry Division remained under the command of Maj. Gen. J.E.B. Stuart.

The Union Army of the Potomac, under Maj. Gen. Joseph Hooker, consisted of seven infantry corps, a cavalry corps, and an Artillery Reserve, for a combined strength of about 94,000 men.

The first major action of the campaign took place on June 9 between cavalry forces at Brandy Station, near Culpeper, Virginia. The 9,500 Confederate cavalrymen under Stuart were surprised by Maj. Gen. Alfred Pleasonton's combined arms force of two cavalry divisions (8,000 troopers) and 3,000 infantry, but Stuart eventually repulsed the Union attack. The inconclusive battle, the largest predominantly cavalry engagement of the war, proved for the first time that the Union horse soldier was equal to his Southern counterpart.

By mid-June, the Army of Northern Virginia was poised to cross the Potomac River and enter Maryland. After defeating the Federal garrisons at Winchester and Martinsburg, Ewell's Second Corps began crossing the river on June 15. Hill's and Longstreet's corps followed on June 24 and 25. Hooker's army pursued, keeping between the U.S. capital and Lee's army. The Federals crossed the Potomac from June 25 to 27.

This 1863 oval-shaped map depicts Gettysburg Battlefield during July 1 to 3, 1863, showing troop and artillery positions and movements, relief hachures, drainage, roads, railroads, and houses with the names of residents at the time of the Battle of Gettysburg.

Lee gave strict orders for his army to minimize any negative impacts on the civilian population. Food, horses, and other supplies were generally not seized outright, although quartermasters reimbursing Northern farmers and merchants with Confederate money were not well received. Various towns, most notably York, Pennsylvania, were required to pay indemnities in lieu of supplies, under threat of destruction. During the invasion, the Confederates seized some 40 northern African Americans. A few of them were escaped fugitive slaves, but most were freemen; all were sent south into slavery under guard.

On June 26, elements of Maj. Gen. Jubal Early's division of Ewell's Corps occupied the town of Gettysburg after chasing off newly raised Pennsylvania militia in a series of minor skirmishes. Early laid the borough under tribute but did not collect any significant supplies. Soldiers burned several railroad cars and a covered bridge, and destroyed nearby rails and telegraph lines. The following morning, General Early departed for adjacent York County.

Meanwhile, in a controversial move, Lee allowed Jeb Stuart to take a portion of the army's cavalry and ride around the east flank of the Union army. Lee's orders gave Stuart much latitude, and both generals share the blame for the long absence of Stuart's cavalry, as well as for the failure to assign a more active role to the cavalry left with the army. Stuart and his three best brigades were absent from the army during the crucial phase of the approach to Gettysburg and the first two days of battle. By June 29, Lee's army was strung out in an arc from Chambersburg (28 miles northwest of Gettysburg) to Carlisle (30 miles north of Gettysburg) to near Harrisburg and Wrightsville on the Susquehanna River.

In a dispute over the use of the forces defending the Harpers Ferry garrison, Hooker offered his resignation, and Abraham Lincoln and General-in-Chief Henry W. Halleck, who were looking for an excuse to get rid of him, immediately accepted. They replaced Hooker early on the morning of June 28 with Maj. Gen. George Gordon Meade, then commander of the V Corps.

On June 29, when Lee learned that the Army of the Potomac had crossed the Potomac River, he ordered a concentration of his forces around Cashtown, located at the eastern base of South Mountain and eight miles west of Gettysburg. On June 30, while part of Hill's Corps was in Cashtown, one of Hill's brigades, North Carolinians under Brig. Gen. J. Johnston Pettigrew, ventured toward Gettysburg. In his memoirs, Maj. Gen. Henry Heth, Pettigrew's division commander, claimed that he sent Pettigrew to search for supplies in town—especially shoes.

When Pettigrew's troops approached Gettysburg on June 30, they noticed Union cavalry under Brig. Gen. John Buford arriving south of town, and Pettigrew returned to Cashtown without engaging them. When Pettigrew told Hill and Heth what he had seen, neither general believed that there was a substantial Federal force in or near the town, suspecting that it had been only Pennsylvania militia. Despite General Lee's order to avoid a general engagement until his entire army was concentrated, Hill decided to mount a significant reconnaissance in force the following morning to determine the size and strength of the enemy force in his front. Around 5 a.m. on Wednesday, July 1, two brigades of Heth's division advanced to Gettysburg.

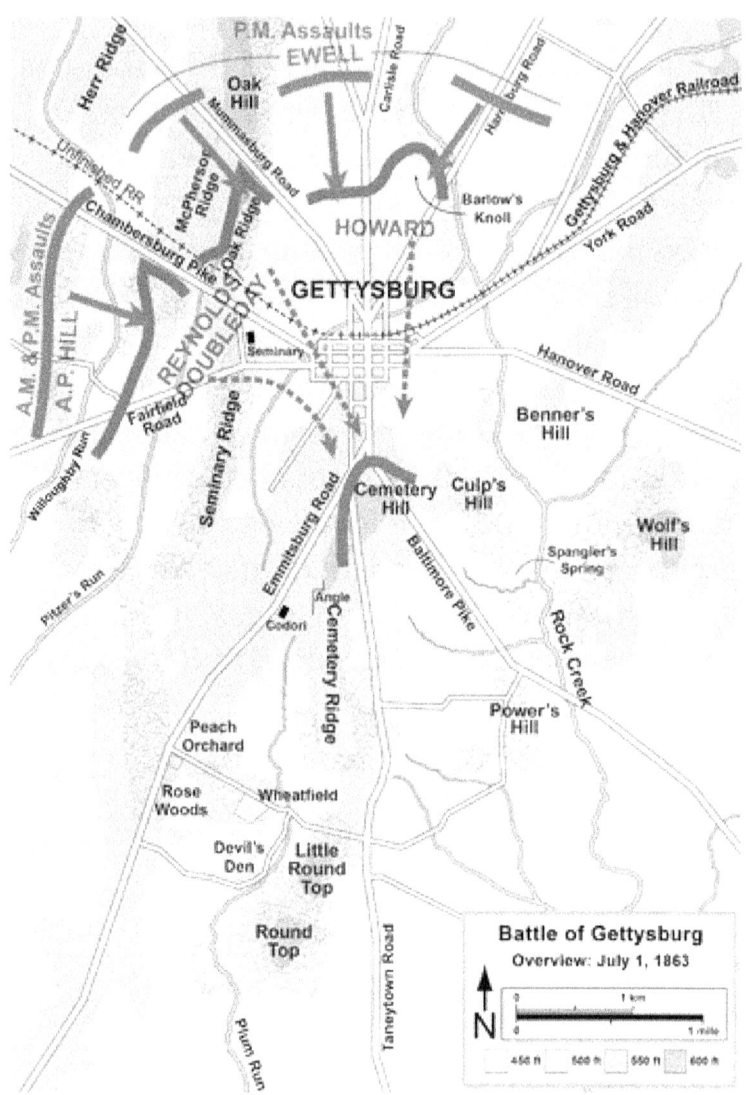

First day of battle

Overview map of the first day of the Battle of Gettysburg, July 1, 1863

Anticipating that the Confederates would march on Gettysburg from the west on the morning of July 1, Buford laid out his defenses on three ridges west of the town: Herr Ridge, McPherson Ridge, and Seminary Ridge. These were appropriate terrain for a delaying action by his small cavalry division against superior Confederate infantry forces, meant to buy time awaiting the arrival of Union infantrymen who could occupy the strong defensive positions south of town at Cemetery Hill, Cemetery Ridge, and Culp's Hill. Buford understood that if the Confederates could gain control of these heights, Meade's army would have difficulty dislodging them.

Heth's division advanced with two brigades forward, commanded by Brig. Generals James J. Archer and Joseph R. Davis. They proceeded easterly in columns along the Chambersburg Pike. Three miles west of town, about 7:30 a.m. on July 1, the two brigades met light resistance from vedettes of Union cavalry, and deployed into line. According to lore, the Union soldier to fire the first shot of the battle was Lt. Marcellus Jones. In 1886 Lt. Jones returned to Gettysburg to mark the spot where he fired the first shot with a monument. Eventually, Heth's men reached dismounted troopers of Col. William Gamble's cavalry brigade, who raised determined resistance and delaying tactics from behind fence posts with fire from their breechloading carbines. Still, by 10:20 a.m., the Confederates had pushed the Union cavalrymen east to McPherson Ridge, when the vanguard of the I Corps (Maj. Gen. John F. Reynolds) finally arrived.

North of the pike, Davis gained a temporary success against Brig. Gen. Lysander Cutler's brigade but was repulsed with heavy losses in an action around an unfinished railroad bed cut in the ridge. South of the pike, Archer's brigade assaulted through Herbst (also known as McPherson's) Woods. The Federal Iron Brigade under Brig. Gen. Solomon Meredith enjoyed initial success against Archer, capturing several hundred men, including Archer himself.

General Reynolds was shot and killed early in the fighting while directing troop and artillery placements just to the east of the woods. Shelby Foote wrote that the Union cause lost a man considered by many to be "the best general in the army." Maj. Gen. Abner Doubleday assumed command. Fighting in the Chambersburg Pike area lasted until about 12:30 p.m. It resumed around 2:30 p.m., when Heth's entire division engaged, adding the brigades of Pettigrew and Col. John M. Brockenbrough.

As Pettigrew's North Carolina Brigade came on line, they flanked the 19th Indiana and drove the Iron Brigade back. The 26th North Carolina (the largest regiment in the army with 839 men) lost heavily, leaving the first day's fight with around 212 men. By the end of the three-day battle, they had about 152 men standing, the highest casualty percentage for one battle of any regiment, North or South. Slowly the Iron Brigade was pushed out of the woods toward Seminary Ridge. Hill added Maj. Gen. William Dorsey Pender's division to the assault, and the I Corps was driven back through the grounds of the Lutheran Seminary and Gettysburg streets.

As the fighting to the west proceeded, two divisions of Ewell's Second Corps, marching west toward Cashtown in accordance with Lee's order for the army to concentrate in that vicinity, turned south on the Carlisle and Harrisburg roads toward Gettysburg, while the Union XI Corps (Maj. Gen. Oliver O. Howard) raced north on the Baltimore Pike and Taneytown Road. By early afternoon, the Federal line ran in a semicircle west, north, and northeast of Gettysburg.

However, the Federals did not have enough troops; Cutler, who was deployed north of the Chambersburg Pike, had his right flank in the air. The leftmost division of the XI Corps was unable to deploy in time to strengthen the line, so Doubleday was forced to throw in reserve brigades to salvage his line.

Around 2 p.m., the Confederate Second Corps divisions of Maj. Gens. Robert E. Rodes and Jubal Early assaulted and out-flanked the Union I and XI Corps positions north and northwest of town. The Confederate brigades of Col. Edward A. O'Neal and Brig. Gen. Alfred Iverson suffered severe losses assaulting the I Corps division of Brig. Gen. John C. Robinson south of Oak Hill. Early's division profited from a blunder by Brig. Gen. Francis C. Barlow, when he advanced his XI Corps division to Blocher's Knoll (directly north of town and now known as Barlow's Knoll); this represented a salient in the corps line, susceptible to attack from multiple sides, and Early's troops overran Barlow's division, which constituted the right flank of the Union Army's position. Barlow was wounded and captured in the attack.

As Federal positions collapsed both north and west of town, Gen. Howard ordered a retreat to the high ground south of town at Cemetery Hill, where he had left the division of Brig. Gen. Adolph von Steinwehr in reserve. Maj. Gen. Winfield S. Hancock assumed command of the battlefield, sent by Meade when he heard that Reynolds had been killed. Hancock, commander of the II Corps and Meade's most trusted subordinate, was ordered to take command of the field and to determine whether Gettysburg was an appropriate place for a major battle. Hancock told Howard, "I think this the strongest position by nature upon which to fight a battle that I ever saw." When Howard agreed, Hancock concluded the discussion: "Very well, sir, I select this as the battle-field." Hancock's determination had a morale-boosting effect on the retreating Union soldiers, but he played no direct tactical role on the first day.

General Lee understood the defensive potential to the Union if they held this high ground. He sent orders to Ewell that Cemetery Hill be taken "if practicable." Ewell, who had previously served under Stonewall Jackson, a general well known for issuing peremptory orders, determined such an assault was not practicable and, thus, did not attempt it; this decision is considered by historians to be a great missed opportunity.

The first day at Gettysburg, more significant than simply a prelude to the bloody second and third days, ranks as the 23rd biggest battle of the war by number of troops engaged. About one quarter of Meade's army (22,000 men) and one third of Lee's army (27,000) were engaged.

Second day of battle

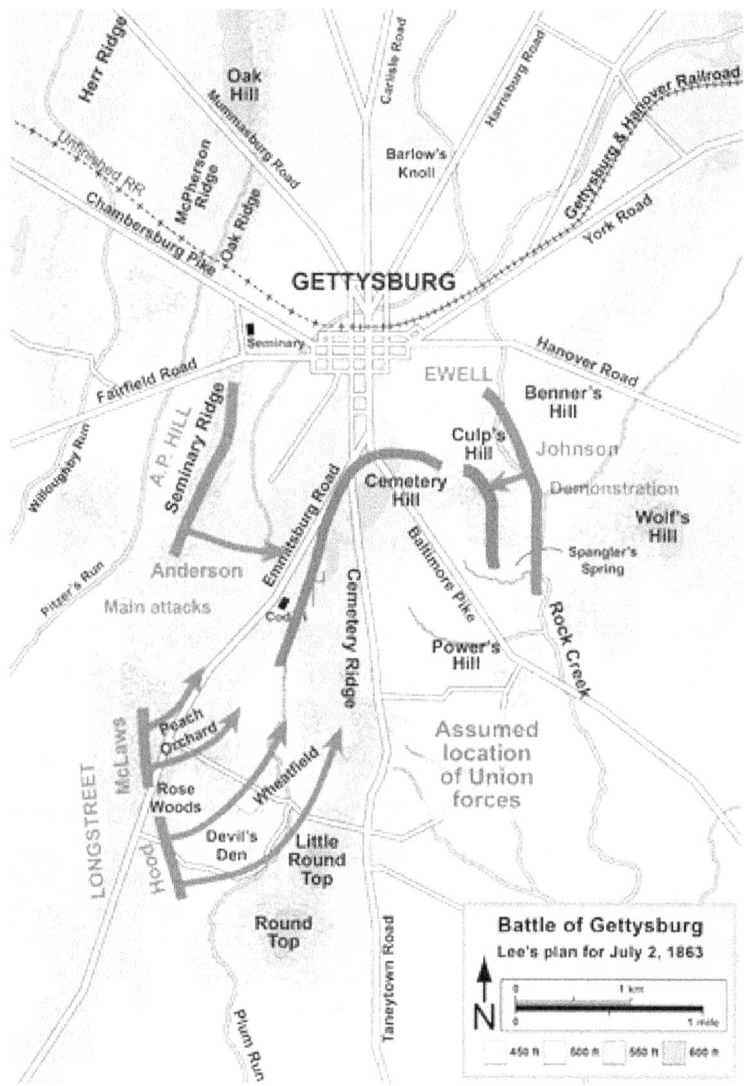

Robert E. Lee's plan for July 2, 1863

Plans and movement to battle.

Throughout the evening of July 1 and morning of July 2, most of the remaining infantry of both armies arrived on the field, including the Union II, III, V, VI, and XII Corps. Longstreet's third division, commanded by Maj. Gen. George Pickett, had begun the march from Chambersburg early in the morning; it did not arrive until late on July 2.

The Union line ran from Culp's Hill southeast of the town, northwest to Cemetery Hill just south of town, then south for nearly two miles along Cemetery Ridge, terminating just north of Little Round Top. Most of the XII Corps was on Culp's Hill; the remnants of I and XI Corps defended Cemetery Hill; II Corps covered most of the northern half of Cemetery Ridge; and III Corps was ordered to take up a position to its flank. The shape of the Union line is popularly described as a "fishhook" formation. The Confederate line paralleled the Union line about a mile (1,600 m) to the west on Seminary Ridge, ran east through the town, then curved southeast to a point opposite Culp's Hill. Thus, the Federal army had interior lines, while the Confederate line was nearly five miles long.

Lee's battle plan for July 2 called for Longstreet's First Corps to position itself stealthily to attack the Union left flank, facing northeast astraddle the Emmitsburg Road, and to roll up the Federal line. The attack sequence was to begin with Maj. Gens. John Bell Hood's and Lafayette McLaws's divisions, followed by Maj. Gen. Richard H.

Anderson's division of Hill's Third Corps. The progressive *en echelon* sequence of this attack would prevent Meade from shifting troops from his center to bolster his left. At the same time, Maj. Gen. Edward "Allegheny" Johnson's and Jubal Early's Second Corps divisions were to make a demonstration against Culp's and Cemetery Hills (again, to prevent the shifting of Federal troops), and to turn the demonstration into a full-scale attack if a favorable opportunity presented itself.

Lee's plan, however, was based on faulty intelligence, exacerbated by Stuart's continued absence from the battlefield. Instead of moving beyond the Federals' left and attacking their flank, Longstreet's left division, under McLaws, would face Maj. Gen. Daniel Sickles's III Corps directly in their path. Sickles had been dissatisfied with the position assigned him on the southern end of Cemetery Ridge. Seeing higher ground more favorable to artillery positions a half mile to the west, he advanced his corps, without orders, to the slightly higher ground along the Emmitsburg Road. The new line ran from Devil's Den, northwest to the Sherfy farm's Peach Orchard, then northeast along the Emmitsburg Road to south of the Codori farm. This created an untenable salient at the Peach Orchard; Brig. Gen. Andrew A. Humphreys's division (in position along the Emmitsburg Road) and Maj. Gen. David B. Birney's division (to the south) were subject to attacks from two sides and were spread out over a longer front than their small corps could defend effectively.

Longstreet's attack was to be made as early as practicable; however, Longstreet got permission from Lee to await the arrival of one of his brigades, and while marching to the assigned position, his men came within sight of a Union signal station on Little Round Top. Countermarching to avoid detection wasted much time, and Hood's and McLaws's divisions did not launch their attacks until just after 4 p.m. and 5 p.m., respectively.

Overview map of the second day of the Battle of Gettysburg, July 2, 1863

As Longstreet's divisions slammed into the Union III Corps, Meade was forced to send 20,000 reinforcements in the form of the entire V Corps, Brig. Gen. John C. Caldwell's division of the II Corps, most of the XII Corps, and small portions of the newly arrived VI Corps. The Confederate assault deviated from Lee's plan since Hood's division moved more easterly than intended, losing its alignment with the Emmitsburg Road, attacking Devil's Den and Little Round Top. McLaws, coming in on Hood's left, drove multiple attacks into the thinly stretched III Corps in the Wheatfield and overwhelmed them in Sherfy's Peach Orchard. McLaws's attack eventually reached Plum Run Valley (the "Valley of Death") before being beaten back by the Pennsylvania Reserves division of the V Corps, moving down from Little Round Top. The III Corps was virtually destroyed as a combat unit in this battle, and Sickles's leg was amputated after it was shattered by a cannonball. Caldwell's division was destroyed piecemeal in the Wheatfield. Anderson's division, coming from McLaws's left and starting forward around 6 p.m., reached the crest of Cemetery Ridge, but it could not hold the position in the face of counterattacks from the II Corps, including an almost suicidal bayonet charge by the small 1st Minnesota regiment against a Confederate brigade, ordered in desperation by Hancock to buy time for reinforcements to arrive.

As fighting raged in the Wheatfield and Devil's Den, Col. Strong Vincent of V Corps had a precarious hold on Little Round Top, an important hill at the extreme left of the Union line. His brigade of four relatively small regiments was able to resist repeated assaults by Brig. Gen. Evander M. Law's brigade of Hood's division. Meade's chief engineer, Brig. Gen. Gouverneur K. Warren, had realized the importance of this position, and dispatched Vincent's brigade, an artillery battery, and the 140th New York to occupy Little Round Top mere minutes before Hood's troops arrived. The defense of Little Round Top with a bayonet charge by the 20th Maine was one of the most fabled episodes in the Civil War and propelled Col. Joshua L. Chamberlain into prominence after the war.

Union breastworks on Culp's Hill

About 7:00 p.m., the Second Corps' attack by Johnson's division on Culp's Hill got off to a late start. Most of the hill's defenders, the Union XII Corps, had been sent to the left to defend against Longstreet's attacks, and the only portion of the corps remaining on the hill was a brigade of New Yorkers under Brig. Gen. George S. Greene. Because of Greene's insistence on constructing

119

strong defensive works, and with reinforcements from the I and XI Corps, Greene's men held off the Confederate attackers, although the Southerners did capture a portion of the abandoned Federal works on the lower part of Culp's Hill.

Just at dark, two of Jubal Early's brigades attacked the Union XI Corps positions on East Cemetery Hill where Col. Andrew L. Harris of the 2nd Brigade, 1st Division, came under a withering attack, losing half his men; however, Early failed to support his brigades in their attack, and Ewell's remaining division, that of Maj. Gen. Robert E. Rodes, failed to aid Early's attack by moving against Cemetery Hill from the west. The Union army's interior lines enabled its commanders to shift troops quickly to critical areas, and with reinforcements from II Corps, the Federal troops retained possession of East Cemetery Hill, and Early's brigades were forced to withdraw.

Jeb Stuart and his three cavalry brigades arrived in Gettysburg around noon but had no role in the second day's battle. Brig. Gen. Wade Hampton's brigade fought a minor engagement with newly promoted 23-year-old Brig. Gen. George Armstrong Custer's Michigan cavalry near Hunterstown to the northeast of Gettysburg.

Third day of battle

Further information: Culp's Hill, Pickett's Charge, and Third Day cavalry battles

General Lee wished to renew the attack on Friday, July 3, using the same basic plan as the previous day: Longstreet would attack the Federal left, while Ewell attacked Culp's Hill. However, before Longstreet was ready, Union XII Corps troops started a dawn artillery bombardment against the Confederates on Culp's Hill in an effort to regain a portion of their lost works. The Confederates attacked, and the second fight for Culp's Hill ended around 11 a.m. Harry Pfanz judged that, after some seven hours of bitter combat, "the Union line was intact and held more strongly than before."

Lee was forced to change his plans. Longstreet would command Pickett's Virginia division of his own First Corps, plus six brigades from Hill's Corps, in an attack on the Federal II Corps position at the right center of the Union line on Cemetery Ridge. Prior to the attack, all the artillery the Confederacy could bring to bear on the Federal positions would bombard and weaken the enemy's line.

The "High Water Mark" on Cemetery Ridge as it appears today. The monument to the 72nd Pennsylvania Volunteer Infantry Regiment ("Baxter's Philadelphia Fire Zouaves") appears at right, the Copse of Trees to the left.

Around 1 p.m., from 150 to 170 Confederate guns began an artillery bombardment that was probably the largest of the war. In order to save valuable ammunition for the infantry attack that they knew would follow, the Army of the Potomac's artillery, under the command of Brig. Gen. Henry Jackson Hunt, at first did not return the enemy's fire. After waiting about 15 minutes, about 80 Federal cannons added to the din. The Army of Northern Virginia was critically low on artillery ammunition, and the cannonade did not significantly affect the Union position. Around 3 p.m., the cannon fire subsided, and 12,500 Southern soldiers stepped from the ridgeline and advanced the three-quarters of a mile to Cemetery Ridge in what is known to history as "Pickett's Charge". As the Confederates approached, there was fierce flanking artillery fire from Union positions on Cemetery Hill and north of Little Round Top, and musket and canister fire from Hancock's II Corps. In the Union center, the commander of artillery had held fire during the Confederate bombardment (in order to save it for the infantry assault, which Meade had correctly predicted the day before), leading Southern commanders to believe the Northern cannon batteries had been knocked out. However, they opened fire on the Confederate infantry during their approach with devastating results. Nearly one half of the attackers did not return to their own lines. Although the Federal line wavered and broke temporarily at a jog called the "Angle" in a low stone fence, just north of a patch of vegetation called the Copse of Trees, reinforcements rushed into the breach, and the Confederate attack was repulsed. The farthest advance of Brig. Gen. Lewis A. Armistead's brigade of Maj. Gen. George Pickett's division at the Angle is referred to as the "High-water mark of the Confederacy", arguably representing the closest the South ever came to its goal of achieving independence from the Union via military victory.

There were two significant cavalry engagements on July 3. Stuart was sent to guard the Confederate left flank and was to be prepared to exploit any success the infantry might achieve on Cemetery Hill by flanking the Federal right and hitting their trains and lines of communications. Three miles east of Gettysburg, in what is now called "East Cavalry Field" (not shown on the accompanying map, but between the York and Hanover Roads), Stuart's forces collided with Federal cavalry: Brig. Gen. David McMurtrie Gregg's division and Brig. Gen. Custer's brigade. A lengthy mounted battle, including hand-to-hand sabre combat, ensued. Custer's charge, leading the 1st Michigan Cavalry, blunted the attack by Wade Hampton's brigade, blocking Stuart from achieving his objectives in the Federal rear. Meanwhile, after hearing news of the day's victory, Brig. Gen. Judson Kilpatrick launched a cavalry attack against the infantry positions of Longstreet's Corps southwest of Big Round Top. Brig. Gen. Elon J. Farnsworth protested against the futility of such a move but obeyed orders. Farnsworth was killed in the attack, and his brigade suffered significant losses.

The Confederates that made it to wall heard the words being shouted, "Fredericksburg" Fredericksburg"!

Some were helped through the line to save their lifes, but would be prisoners of war.

Chapter 17
The Retreat

The Confederate Army of Northern Virginia began its **Retreat from Gettysburg** on July 4, 1863. Following General Robert E. Lee's failure to defeat the Union Army at the Battle of Gettysburg (July 1–3, 1863), he ordered a retreat through Maryland and over the Potomac River to relative safety in Virginia. The Union Army of the Potomac, commanded by Maj. Gen. George G. Meade, was unable to maneuver quickly enough to launch a significant attack on the Confederates, who crossed the river on the night of July 13 to 14.

Confederate supplies and thousands of wounded men proceeded over South Mountain through Cashtown in a wagon train that extended for 15 to 20 miles, enduring harsh weather, treacherous roads, and enemy cavalry raids. The bulk of Lee's infantry departed through Fairfield and through the Monterey Pass toward Hagerstown, Maryland. Reaching the Potomac, they found that rising waters and destroyed pontoon bridges prevented their immediate crossing. Erecting substantial defensive works, they awaited the arrival of the Union army, which had been pursuing over longer roads more to the south of Lee's route. Before Meade could perform adequate reconnaissance and attack the Confederate fortifications, Lee's army escaped across fords and a hastily rebuilt bridge. Combat operations, primarily cavalry battles, raids, and skirmishes, occurred during the retreat at Fairfield (July 3), Monterey Pass (July 4 to 5), Smithsburg (July 5), Hagerstown (July 6 and 12), Boonsboro (July 8), Funkstown (July 7 and 10), and around Williamsport and Falling Waters (July 6 to 14). Additional clashes after the armies crossed the Potomac occurred at Shepherdstown (July 16) and Manassas Gap (July 23) in Virginia, ending the Gettysburg Campaign of June and July 1863.

The Brigade of General Corse had been guarding Richmond, so they had a forced march to meet General Lee and escort them back to Virginia. The 29th Virginia Infantry helped clear the gaps of all Yankee opposition.

The Confederate Army's rear guard arrived in Hagerstown on the morning of July 7, screened skillfully by their cavalry, and began to establish defensive positions. By July 11 they occupied a 6-mile line on high ground with their right resting on the Potomac River near Downsville and the left about 1.5 miles southwest of Hagerstown, covering the only road from there to Williamsport. The Conococheague Creek protected the position from any attack that might be launched from the west. They erected impressive earthworks with a 6-foot-wide parapet on top and frequent gun emplacements, creating comprehensive crossfire zones. Longstreet's Corps occupied the right end of the line, Hill's the center, and Ewell's the left. These works were completed on the morning of July 12, just as the Union army arrived to confront them.

The bloody struggle 1861 to 1865

The rear guard was made up of General Alfred Iverson's infantry and they would stand off the Yankee pursuit. It was important to hold Hagerstown so that General Lee could get all of his supplies and men across the Potomac. He had a wagon train up to twenty-five miles long with wounded, extra supplies, cannon and ammunition.

Colonel Alexander Phipps brought a dispatch to General Iverson from General Lee. The dispatch ordered General Iverson to hold Hagerstown at all cost.

After Colonel Phipps gave General Iverson the dispatch, he asked if he could join the fray, because at that time the Southern Army was getting pushed back. With permission given, he sent Prancer down the street with a slap on his behind. Colonel Phipps felt compelled to help in this critical fight. Colonel Phipps was an expert sharpshooter with his 44 caliber Navy Colt. The fight was from street to street building-to-building and much hand to hand combat. Colonel Phipps took aim at the first blue coat he saw and squeezed the trigger. The ball found the mark and the Yankee crumpled to the ground. Then here come more, there were four leading a little charge toward him. He fired 1, 2, 3, and 4. Three Yankee's fell to the earth one was grazed and took cover.

General Lee, and Traveler

Now many more Yankees come down the street, and Colonel Phipps had two shots left. Now a company of Confederates comes up to fight with the Colonel. They saw the Colonel and accepted him Colonel Phipps shot twice more and two more Yankees fell, but one jumped up, turned, and ran back up the street. Colonel Phipps led the Confederates up the street being entirely too brave. The company of Gray-backs let loose with their muskets and the charge reversed into a retreat. They were determined to send the Yankees to hell or at least running tuck-tail back north.

Shots were still coming from the Yankees and two balls hit the Colonel. One in his shoulder and one in the fleshier part of his upper leg, and one other ball went through his sleeve with not more than a scrape. Colonel Phipps fell and he was immediately carried out of harms way to the medical area.

Thank God, no bones were hit and he will have a full recovery in a few weeks. There were several wounded men there and Colonel Phipps said, "Doctor help those men with the worse wounds first."
The doctor smiled, as he made sure he stopped the bleeding on the Colonel.

Colonel Phipps shot twice more and two more Yankees fell, but one jumped up, turned, and ran back up the street. Colonel Phipps led the Confederates up the street being entirely too brave. The company of Gray-backs let loose with their muskets and the charge reversed into a retreat. They were determined to send the Yankees to hell or at least running tuck-tail back north.

Shots were still coming from the Yankees and two balls hit the Colonel. One in his shoulder and one in the fleshier part of his upper leg, and one other ball went through his sleeve with not more than a scrape. Colonel Phipps fell and he was immediately carried out of harms way to the medical area.

Thank God, no bones were hit and he will have a full recovery in a few weeks. There were several wounded men there and Colonel Phipps said, "Doctor help those men with the worse wounds first."

The doctor smiled, as he made sure he stopped the bleeding on the Colonel.

The bloody surgeon told Colonel Phipps he was very lucky, no amputations for him. He told Colonel Phipps he would be weak for a while because he had lost much blood, so take it easy. He told Colonel Phipps he was lucky that the balls had not hit a bone and there would be no amputations needed.

Rendition of Confederate rear guard repelling the Yankees.

The beautifully dressed were not seen much during the last years of the war.

Finally, the Yankees had had enough so they gave up on Hagers Town and withdrew.

It was like a miracle, John Livingston was there when the fighting started and had hidden out in one of the buildings.

When John came out, he recognized Colonel Phipps and ran to check on him. After talking to him and seeing the need for someone to take care of him, he asked General Iverson if he could take the Colonel to his home until he was well enough to return to duty. The General agreed and actually thought it a good idea. They made a bed of blankets on straw in a wagon and laid the Colonel in it. John Livingston had to go by the William Adams plantation on the way to his home to stay off the main roads.

As John Livingston nears the Adams Plantation, the Adams' all including Hannah ran to see John and ask about the raging battle in Hagers Town. John pulled up to give them a report.

He said, "The battle is over and the Confederates held off the Union, and control our town. I think that it was just to buy time so Lee could get his army back to the safety across the Potomac River."

All of the Adams' were up close to the stopped wagon. William, Martha, Hannah, Archibald, Mary Jane, and

Ginger gathered around the wagon; they were holding on to the side to hear what John Livingston had to say.

Of course, the wounded Colonel Alexander Phipps was under the tarp so that he would not be detected. About that time Alex moved the tarp just a little and moaned with pain. Hannah saw the movement of the tarp and asked, "Mister Wellington Sir, what is under the canvas tarp?"

John answered, "Might as well tell you, I have a wounded soldier in my wagon."

"I aim to take him home so he can recover," said John Wellington.

"He is hurt bad, he was shot in the shoulder and upper leg and cannot walk. He needs tender care for a few weeks so he can mend up," explained John Wellington.

Ginger the always forward and curious one yanked back the canvas before anyone could say a word. There he was Colonel Alexander Phipps in a duty gray uniform with blood all over it.

They all stood there in amazement to see Alex as a Colonel in the Confederate army and also to see the pain stricken face with dirt and blood all over him.

Chapter 18

The Secreat Is Revealed

Hannah screamed, "It's my Alex; get him out of the wagon and in to the house!"

"But I aim to take him to my house until he mends," said John Livingston.

"No, No, get him in the house and I will nurse him back to health, "exclaimed Hannah.

Ginger spoke up quickly, "I shall help her."

William Adams looked at John expectantly and said, "Well John if you don't have any objection we will take this young man into the house and let the ladies take care of him.

"Reckon that will be fine, long as you think it's okay, William," said John.

"Please be prepared to keep this quiet, some folks around here would as soon as shoot him as not," said John.

"Well let me drive the wagon close to the house so we don't have to carry him too far," said John.

"Good idea, I will take Archibald over to the barn, we have a stretcher over in the tool shed just in case," Said William.

"Please hurry, he sure needs some attention," piped up Hannah.

Rendition of the William Adams House.

Jefferson Davis

President of the Confederates States of America

1861-1865

John drove over to the house and William and Archibald came walking briskly from the barn with the stretcher.

Alex was hurting bad, but felt relieved that his status as a Confederate soldier was accepted by the Adams family and especially Hannah.

Martha ran in the house and had her House Girl get water on to boil and then she gathered up clean linen for fresh bandages. Then her and Mary Jane went upstairs and made the bed and room ready.

Archibald and Mary Jane had been sleeping there but now since the battles have subsided, they would go back home. Ginger can room with Hannah, they both can sit, and care for him was the thinking.

By now, the wounds had stiffened Alex up and he had some real pain. The main thing was that he had stopped bleeding. He was still lying in the wagon almost unconscious when he heard the people around him again.

"Alex, Alex, you ready to go to the house and get in a real bed?" asked William.

Alex raised his head and could see William through the lowered tailgate of the wagon.

"Yes Sir, I reckon so now is as good as any," replied Alex in a weak voice.

Gathering the Wounded after Battle

Tending the wounded and sick.

Rendition of Wounded Soldiers at Hagerstown

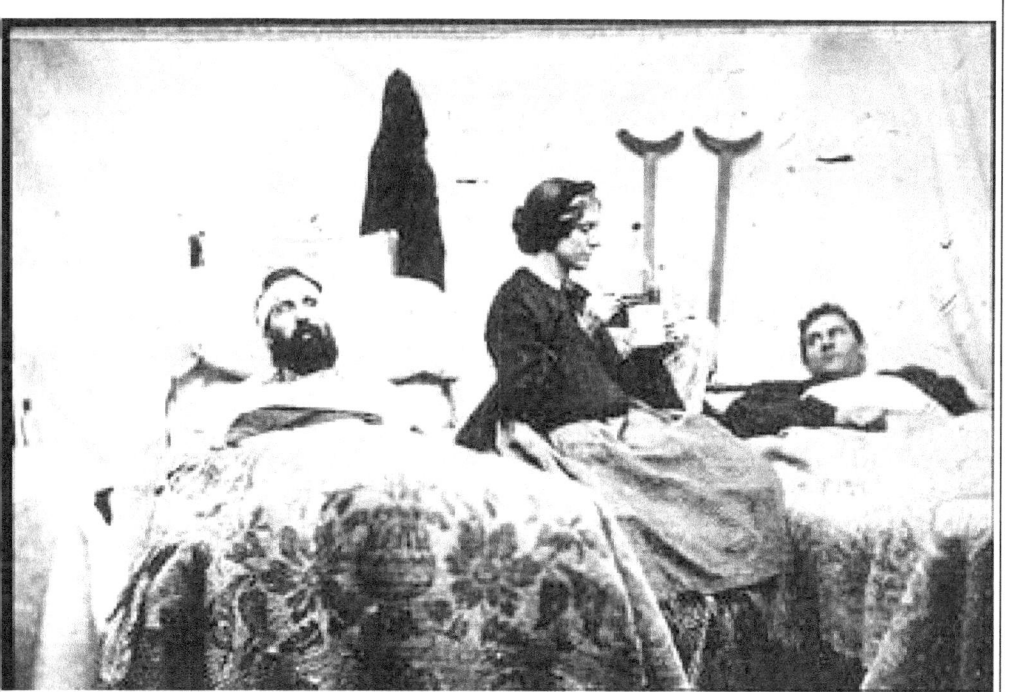

A confederate and a Union soldier side by side.

General U.S. Grant

North side of Hagerstown 1863, notice the Ambulances

Then Alex spoke again, "Sir I am so thirsty can I have a drink of water?" Pleaded Alex.

"Alex, take a little drink of the spirits first, it will help you with the pain. Alex took a little drink and it was hot in his mouth and throat, but not bad after he swallowed.

"Damn," exclaimed Alex before he could think.
John and William both laughed and John said, "Colonel, you are going to be just fine."

Hannah kinda scolded the men for giving Alex the strong spirits. William turned to her and said, "Sweet Hannah, we are doing what's best for him, it will be easier to move him with some spirits in him."

"You shall have all the water you want Alex, just as soon as we carry you upstairs to your bed," answered William.
Archibald whispered to William, "It's the loss of blood, it always makes you thirsty."

Now four young slaves were brought out and were made ready to carry Alex upstairs. They picked him up so easy and their strength made it easy to carry him. They were told to keep him level even going up the steps and Alex had a smooth ride all the way to the bed. After the four black men laid him in the bed, Alex smiled at then and thanked them.

Water was brought to him to drink and as soon as he had his water, Hannah began getting his bloody, dirty uniform off.

Rendition of the Confederate Retreat through Hagers Town.

"The Gray Fox."

General Robert Edward Lee

Many Fine Horses Died in the War

She was so gentle and as soon as she washed his face, she bent down and kissed his lips softly.

Hannah took warm water and soap and gently washed Alex as she removed his clothes. This brought him to full consciousness and he smiled at Hannah.

Hannah smiled back at him and said, "Colonel, I am so proud of you!"

He looked into her beautiful eyes and asked, "Why, Why Hannah are you proud of me?"

"You are my brave soldier that defends the South from the Yankee intruders," she answered.

"Darling I thought you and your family were for the North," he answered.

"You know I gave you information about what the Union Army was up to," she said.

Hannah continued to clean Alex, and after his upper half was finished, she poured on the homemade corn liquor and then some olive oil. Then she bandaged up the wounds front and back on his shoulder. Then she helped him put on a clean soft shirt.

Hannah gave him more liquor to drink and said, "I have to do your bottom now."

He smiled at her and said, "Be careful,

Oh! I feel funny," then he laughed.

Hannah knew the liquor was taking effect.

Olive Oil as a Medicine

Little Brown Jug of Spirits

Rendition of Pickett's Charge as seen from the Union side at the wall.

Confederates on Defense

Union Calvary hitting the Confederate Rear Guard.

"Silly man it's the corn liquor working on you," answered Hannah.

Then she removed the dirty, bloody pants with the bullet hole through it from front to back. Then she laid a washcloth over his private parts and removed his long drawers.
She washed him from the bottom of his feet to his washcloth-covered parts. Next, she cleaned the leg wound with clear corn liquor and poured on the olive oil. Then she bandaged his upper leg very careful. Next, she put on a pair of her father's long drawers up to the washcloth.

Next she un-covered his private member and washed it and his crotch all the way back to his anus. With the water making noise, he became about to pee.

Alex looked at Hannah and said, "You are my beautiful angel."

Alex said," I need to drink some more water, and I am afraid I need to pee."

Hannah gave him a cup of water and then asked, "Darling can you sit up if I help you?'

"It will hurt like hell but yes I must," he answered.

Hannah gently lifted his back as she brought his legs around. He was sitting up and ready to urinate.

Hannah brought a flower vase and He spread his legs just a bit. Then asked in a loving way, "Can you do it now?"

Old Flower Vases Make fine Urinals.

"Now there you are go ahead and pee," she said.
He discharged a strong yellow urine and felt much relief.

Hannah said, In a motherly way, "Are you done?"

"I reckon so," he said kinda timid.

Hannah smiled and took his member in her fingers and
shook off the dribbles and Alex giggled.

Hannah had just got him back in bed when someone
knocked on the door.

"Come on in," Hollered Hannah.
Ginger opened the door and brought in a bowl of hot
chicken soup. She looked at the dirty uniform and
underwear on the floor and smiled at Hannah.

"Well Colonel you ready to eat some good ole chicken
soup?" she asked?"

"Well I reckon I can try," answered Alex.

Hannah said, "I am going to take these soiled clothes
down and if you don't mind. Ginger please start feeding
him a spoon at a time."
Ginger fed Alex the soup a spoon at a time and never
mentioned the time she lured him out of the ball and
made great advances toward him.

Ginger was going to be the perfect little angel, at least for now.

Civil War Era Chamber Pot or Slop Jar

Alex was made as comfortable as possible and the summer night was falling. Colonel Alexander Phipps had a day to remember.

Hannah set up a rocking chair and would sit the night with him, maybe if she were tired enough she would allow Ginger to sit the next night.

He was receiving Tender Loving Care from the two Adams Ladies.

General Lee was able to get his entire Army across the Potomac River. The Army of Northern Virginia would only face small skirmishes in the gaps. The 29th Virginia was leading them back to safety and clearing the gaps for their brave Confederate Army.

Warrages in Hagerstown

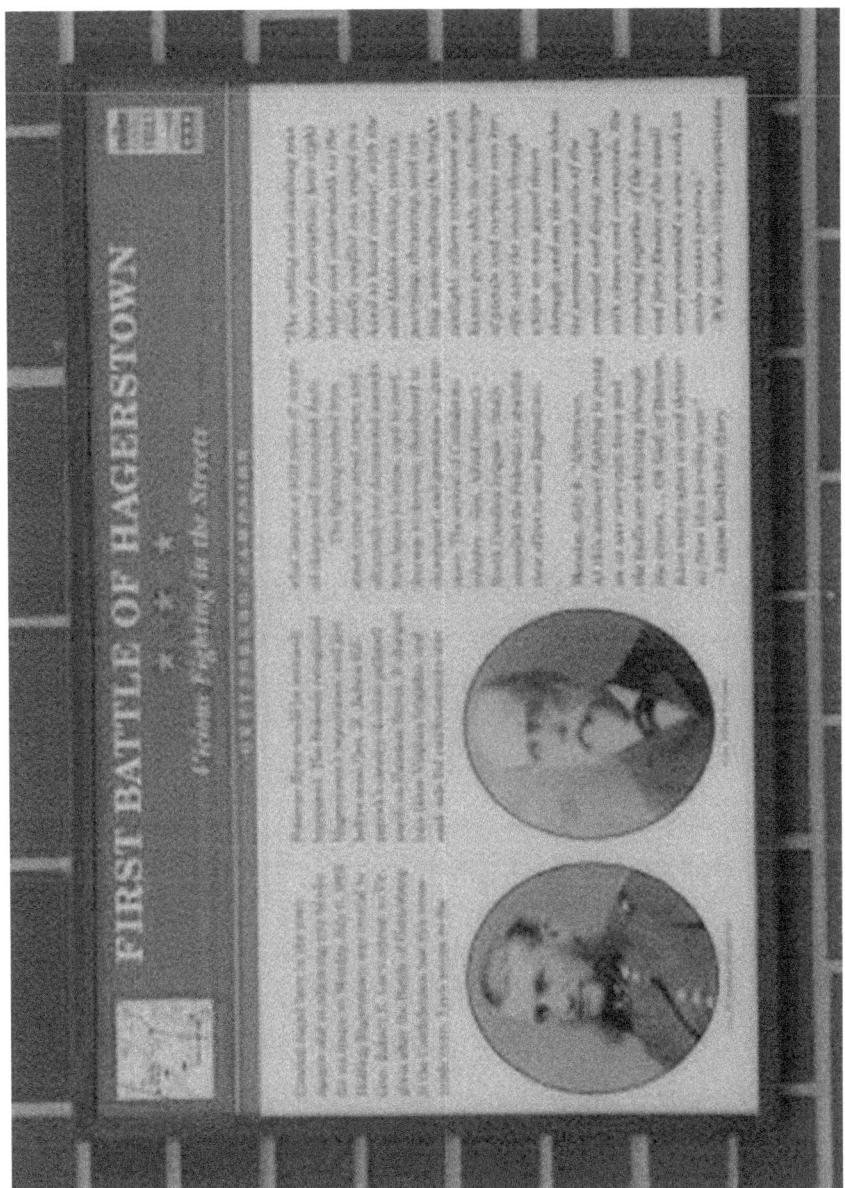

Chapter 19

The Account of the Battle of Hagerstown

On July 6, 1863, Confederate and Union cavalry clashed at the intersection of Baltimore and South Potomac streets in Hagerstown.

That skirmish was the start of what was to become the Battle of Hagerstown, a seven-hour fight that involved roughly 2,000 soldiers and resulted in nearly 200 casualties.

Stephen Bockmiller, a local historian and planner for the City of Hagerstown, said the battle was fought primarily by cavalry troops who crossed paths three days after the Battle of Gettysburg ended July 3.

As the Confederates were retreating on July 4, a driving rainstorm struck the area and caused the Potomac River to swell, Bockmiller said.

The high water, coupled with the Union army's destruction of a Confederate pontoon bridge near Williamsport, produced a barrier that prevented Southern forces from escaping to Virginia.

"The Confederates pretty much find that they're

163

trapped north of the Potomac River," Bockmiller said.

The stage for the Battle of Hagerstown was set when Union Brig. Gen. Hugh Kilpatrick turned his men toward Hagerstown after receiving intelligence that Confederate supply wagons were heading toward the city.

Bockmiller said when Kilpatrick's forces arrived around noon on July 6, they discovered the Rebels already had occupied the town.

"(Kilpatrick) finds that the Confederates have beaten him here," Bockmiller said.

The first phase of the battle started at about noon when a brigade of Virginia cavalry under Col. John Chambliss deployed south of Hagerstown.

The 9th Virginia Cavalry was sent out as skirmishers across the southern end of town, while the 10th Virginia Cavalry formed a barricade along Baltimore Street in the area of South Potomac Street.

"They literally turned over wagons like the stuff you see in old Western movies ... to keep the Union cavalry from getting into town," Bockmiller said.

Union soldiers under the command of Kilpatrick charged several squadrons up Frederick Street. They then turned west on Baltimore Street toward the defending Confederates.

"A fight ensues at the corner of Potomac and Baltimore," Bockmiller said. "The Union cavalry overwhelms the barricade and sends the 9th and 10 Virginia fleeing up Potomac Street near Public Square."

As the two armies clashed on Public Square, a separate company of Confederate cavalry under the command of Capt. Frank Bond joined the fight from Washington Street.

"There was a huge mounted cavalry battle in the middle of Public Square — picture scores and scores of mounted soldiers shooting and slashing at one another," Bockmiller said. "It was pretty much chaos. It was stirrup-to-stirrup action."

During the fight, Bockmiller said, a Confederate sergeant named Hammond Dorsey killed several Union soldiers during a sword battle. Bockmiller said Dorsey's rampage was halted when he went after a Union bugler, who used his instrument to blunt a number of saber strikes from Dorsey.

Witness accounts said the bugle, which was mangled in the attack, saved the Union trooper's life and no doubt spared several of his comrades from Dorsey's wrath.

While the cavalry battle waged on the square, Confederate forces set up more defensive positions to the north near the site of the current City Hall at 1 E. Franklin St. and at Zion Church on the northwest corner of Church and North Potomac streets.

During the third phase of the battle, things slowed down as far as the cavalry action, and Union soldiers hunkered down on Public Square, basically just holding the ground.

Bockmiller said two regiments of North Carolina cavalry under the command of Brig. Gen. Beverly Robertson entered town from the north and created a defensive position at Zion Church.

"The hill that Zion Church is on was the north end of town at the time. It was high ground," Bockmiller said.

He said a few hundred of Robertson's men created the defensive position at Church and Potomac streets.

During this phase of the battle, Bockmiller said, an artillery duel took place.

Union troops set up two artillery pieces at the site of the old Washington County Hospital, he said. At the time, the land was occupied by a school known as the

Hagerstown Female Seminary.

Bockmiller said Confederate artillery deployed on the north end of the city, possibly in the area where Pangborn Elementary School is today.

He said the artillery battle lasted for a 30-minute span that town residents said "shook the town to its core."

Federal artillery hit a Confederate supply wagon loaded with ordnance, Bockmiller said, causing a "huge explosion."

After the artillery exchange, Union troops who earlier had taken up a position on the square divided into two groups of 10 men each.

The men started to move north up both sides of Potomac Street, led by Capt. Ulric Dahlgren, who stayed on top of his horse.

Bockmiller said the Union troops used crates and the insets of doors for cover as they moved up the street.

During the advance, an older man, whose was a civilian and name is not known for certain, exited a building with a musket and joined the fight on the side of the Union.

"He was shot down before he got a block," Bockmiller said.

The Union soldiers were able to make it to Potomac and Franklin streets near the current City Hall.

Meanwhile, the Confederates used alleys to work their way from Zion Church to a well at the site where the Pioneer Ladder Co. on West Franklin Street is today. From there, the Rebels fired at the advancing Yankees.

At the intersection of Franklin and Potomac streets, Dahlgren was shot in the ankle, Bockmiller said. From that point on, the Union advance wavered.

"Dahlgren rides back to Kilpatrick and informs him that we've picked up an extra block of territory, but the attack has stalled down again," Bockmiller said.

Dahlgren, not knowing how badly he was wounded, passed out from losing a large amount of blood. His foot was amputated at Boonsboro shortly after the battle.

Dahlgren returned to action and eventually was promoted to colonel. He died on March 2, 1864, while fighting near Richmond, Va.

The fifth phase of the battle was a mounted Union cavalry charge up Potomac Street toward the Confederate positions at the north end of town.

Bockmiller said the 18th Pennsylvania Cavalry sent two companies up Potomac Street, but the attack fizzled in front of City Hall.

At this point of the battle, Kilpatrick decided that the Confederate supply wagons he initially came to Hagerstown to capture weren't worth the cost.

"What he's got himself into isn't worth trying to get those wagons anymore," Bockmiller said.

Kilpatrick heard that Union Brig. Gen. John Buford was engaged in a fight at Williamsport, and pulled out of Hagerstown at about 7 p.m. to lend support.

"That leaves a battle with a few hundred killed and wounded, and streets littered with dead and wounded men and horses," Bockmiller said.

About 100 Union soldiers were stranded in town when Kilpatrick pulled out, Bockmiller said. A few were able to escape and rejoin their units, while the rest were hidden by residents who were sympathetic to the Union cause.

Bockmiller said one such case was Antipas Curtis, a trooper who served with the 1st Vermont Cavalry.

He said Curtis was given civilian clothes by his hosts.

"He actually went out and walked about town among the Confederate soldiers who occupied the town," Bockmiller said. "The Confederates just see him as a civilian. They don't think anything of it."

Legend has it that Curtis was standing on the street and saluted Gen. Robert E. Lee when the Confederate commander rode past on his horse.

"The lore in the 1st Vermont Cavalry is he was the only man in the regiment who saluted Robert E. Lee," Bockmiller said.

Bockmiller said he believes Curtis didn't give a military salute, but tipped his hat to avoid raising suspicion.

Chapter 20

The Colonel Heals

As time went on, each day there were remarkable differences in Alex. He was healing up nicely. He enjoyed the tender loving care he got from Hannah and Ginger. Ginger had been nice not to infringe on Hannah's rights as a romantic companion to Alex, but she was becoming attached to Alex in a romantic way.

Ginger began to flirt with Alex again after a couple of weeks. She loved to help him pee even though Hannah told her firmly all the private doings was for her to handle.

Alex was sitting up every day now after two weeks, the family Doctor had made calls and directed the ladies how to take care of the wounds. Therefore, Alex began walking around with the help of a crutch William made him. He could now use the Slop Jar by the bed to relieve himself. The House Servants would take it out often and wash it out for Alex.

Alex loved to see the newspapers, even though the North slanted the news to make it look better for the Union. Alex was anxious to get back to his duties in the Confederate Army, but the Doctor and all the Adams' had warned him not to hurry the healing process.

The news in the north had made the battle of Gettysburg a great victory for the north. The history books still do this, but in reality, General Lee escaped with a wagon train several miles long with goods they had salvaged from the fat of the northland. Some folks say it was twenty-six miles long, even though some wagons carried wounded soldiers.

Colonel Alex knew it was a setback, but the spirited Army of Northern Virginia was still intact and ready to defend Dixie Land.

Now that Alex was feeling better and mending up, he began to play and tease with the ladies. He felt he loved Hannah and wanted to marry her, but that hot Ginger was so intriguing.

Alex thought about all that had occurred on that day in Hagerstown and realized how lucky he was not to be dead, or maybe have lost a leg or arm.

Colonel Phipps also read about Vicksburg falling and that would turn the Mississippi River over to the Union. A drinking Union General had won that battle and now had the name of "Unconditional Surrender Grant." Grant made an impression on Abe Lincoln and he would be moving up the ladder of command.

People in the north were so tired of war, even though they had good victories this summer of 1863. On July 13 through the 16th, the folks in New York protested the draft. They murdered Negroes and caused damage of two million dollars. Over 120 folks died in the riots. General Lee saw all of this and felt like if the South could hang on until the election in the north, Abe Lincoln would be cast out, and someone against the war would be in power.

Of course, General Lee got his army back to Virginia and they were preparing for more defense.

Finally, Alex makes it down the spiral staircase and ventures outside where the August sun could shine on him. He would now spend much time out in the gazebo with his Hannah, and sometimes Ginger would horn in. Isn't that what a Horney cousin is supposed to do?

Hannah was annoyed with Ginger and began to thank her for all her help, but don't you think you should go home now?

Anytime Ginger could catch Alex by himself, she would sweet talk him and actually talk about sexual encounters. She would rub her full breast on him, touch him on his leg and sometimes feel his rising member through his pants. Alex struggled with this because Ginger was so beautiful and she did cause him to be aroused. Hannah sensed this and knew Ginger had to go.

173

Hannah went to her mother Martha and explained the situation to her and asked for help. Martha would go to her sister-in-law Mary Jane and get her help to get Ginger back home.

Another day and night Ginger went back home and left Alex to Hannah. Now they could be in private and talk, and even kiss without any intrusions. Hannah had a full-blown love for Alex and he loved her. They began to talk of marriage, but Alex told her it would be best to wait until the war ended because he didn't want to take the chance of making her a widow again. Hannah had other ideas, she felt like if she could have him for her own for a time now and then would be better than not at all.

Once again, Hannah would join him at night after he was able to function without a nurse. Now she would slip to his room and make love to him, but no penetration was allowed. Alex was still sore in his shoulder and in his right upper leg but that did not hinder his member rising up and becoming hard as a rock. Hannah knew how to make it rise. They lay together naked and let their bodies touch skin-to-skin most every night. Hannah knew he was sore in his leg and shoulder so she stumbled on a good idea. Alex liked the idea so they tried it. Hannah would squat on Alex's face placing her sweet bottom lips on Alex's face, then bend down, and take Alex's hard member in her mouth and both could enjoy the wonderful expression of sex without getting pregnant.

Alex knew he must have this beautiful loving Lady for his wife. She had nursed him back to health and he knew she would stand by him through thick and thin. That is what a wife does and a husband also. Once they take, their vows in marriage neither can love another.

Ginger knows about taking oaths and the honor of the marriage bedroom, if she is going to have Alex, she had better start working on it.

News came from the south about the battle of Chickamauga. With the Mississippi river open Union General William S. Rosccerns invaded northern Georgia and Southern Tennessee.

On September 19th and 20th 1863 The Confederate General Braxton Bragg's Army of Tennessee defeated General Rosccerns' army at Chickamauga and left the his union army trapped in Chattanooga, Tennessee.

Abe Lincoln appoints General U.S.Grant to command the Union Army in the western theater of the war. Some folks complained about U.S. Grant's drinking problem, but Lincoln said I will send all my general's whiskey if that is what it takes.

No date for a wedding is set yet, but it is time that Colonel Alexander Phipps rode out on Prancer and went to General Lee for orders.

Ginger knew he would be leaving so she sent him a note to meet her at an abandon house on his way south. He got the note and had second thoughts about meeting her, but decided to see what she wanted of him.

After leaving Hannah in tears, he went to the old farmhouse. Sure enough, Ginger was there. She had driven herself in the buggy and was waiting in the shade of a large oak.

Alex rode Prancer up close to the buggy and Ginger asked him to help her down. He tied Prancer to the buggy, took her beautiful hand, and helped her to the ground. She threw her arms around him and pulled him to her lips.

She immediately had a hand on his member touching it through his pants. It swelled up instantly while she held him in a kiss. They came up for air, and then she took his hand and ran it down into her low-cut top. His hand touched her full breasts and he found a nipple.

Nothing was being said; just hot passion was taking place. Next Ginger freed his hard organ from the restraints of his pants and gripped it and jacking it back and forth.

Alex raised his eyes and looked for a secluded place and Ginger knew what he was thinking. She took him by the hand and led him inside the old house. Ginger had an old bed made up with good clean quilts.

Alex knew without a doubt that Ginger had planned the whole meeting and was going to have him unless he broke and ran. Then he thought about the scorn that may materialize if she was mad, ran back, and told folks he raped her.

Ginger was dropping her clothes left and right as she kissed him between each piece she dropped, Alex began getting out of his clothes and before he knew what happened he was on the bed and the hot, beautiful Ginger was laying on him skin to skin. Her hot wet treasure was rubbing against his hard member and her hot breast were against his chest.

Finally, Ginger spoke up, "I want you in me Alex!"

"What if you get in a family way, I am going to marry Hannah," he said.

"Not today you are not you need to be in me now," she said as she took her hand and guided him into her hot wet cavity of love.

Ohhhhh! Both moaned as he filled her with his hard member and she began to pump him while he sucked her ample breasts.

Things did not last long after that he ejaculated into her, the throbbing beast caused a giant orgasm, and she screamed with ecstasy.

Alex knew he had done wrong and pushed her off him and got her to stand up so his hot seed would drain out quickly. He wiped her and him with a big handkerchief.

"Damn Ginger it was wonderful, I just pray you don't get knocked up," Alex exclaimed.

"According to my calculations I should be safe today, you don't really want Hannah do you?" she asked.
"Yes I do, you are so beautiful but I could never trust you if you were my wife," he said.

Ginger puckered up and cried big tears.
Then she said, "Marry me I will be true to you!"

"Sorry Ginger I am betrothed to Hannah and I will marry her if I survive this war!" He said sternly.

He kissed her on the cheek, mounted Prancer, and rode off with her standing there half dressed. He felt so guilty.

She felt so satisfied, but then so hurt. She now hated and loved Alex.

Rendition of Ginger
By permission of Gloria Nikki Bell

Chapter 21
Back to War

Alexander Phipps was heading back south to meet up with the army. He stopped a couple of times to take orders from Mercantiles and wired the orders in. now he had something in his pocket he could show if stopped by the Yankees and something in his boot to show the Confederate patrols if stopped.

His battle wounds still hurt some and he was out of shape from being laid up for so long, but he was young and his manly strength would come back. As he rode, he often talked to his horse, Prancer. He felt better if he ran things by him and Prancer seemed to listen and sometimes disagree. Today he was thinking about the woman he loved and the one for which he had lust. Then the old guilt feeling would come back for not being true to his sweet Hannah. Then he considered Hannah, there were no better lover than her, why would he give in to lust and lay with Ginger? Then the thought of dread would enter his head, what if she was knocked up?

Colonel Phipps made it back to the army and met with General Lee. General Lee was cordial as usual and asked about his wounds. Colonel Phipps wondered how the high commander knew he was hurt.

General Lee said, "Colonel I heard what you did back in Hagerstown, the South is beholding to you."

Colonel Phipps smiled and thanked General Lee. Then he asked the General how he might best serve him now? General Lee asked if he was fit for duty now and if so he wanted him to go back north again and find out all the news and information about the enemy that he could. Make it a quick trip if you can because you have proven your worthiness as a leader.

 "You will be needed to defend the cause," General Lee instructed.

"General Lee, Sir I am healed up and ready to serve you and the cause, "answered Colonel Phipps.

"I will rest here tonight and Prancer will carry me north on the morrow Sir," said Colonel Phipps.

The next morning it was back to being a drummer and getting orders as he traveled in Yankee Land. He talked to contacts, he asked questions, and even from all he met he gleaned information. He even went near the capital of the United States, Washington D. C. and got newspapers. There was a new sense of urgency in the north either to let the south go or to defeat them quickly.

One thing of importance he noted was that Abe Lincoln had him a General that drink like a fish and did not have sense to back down. Colonel Phipps thought it over and guessed that Grant would end up over the whole Union Army before long.

Colonel Phipps wanted to go by and see Hannah, but this time he was following orders from General Lee himself. Those orders were to make it a quick trip so he trotted Prancer often on his way back to the Army of Northern Virginia.

It was getting way up in the fall when Colonel Phipps met up with the Army of Northern Virginia. He noticed several cold mornings on the way back and some left a heavy coat of frost on the grass. He had more bad news for the General, but he has already heard.

The news was in the northern newspapers. Big headlines that General U.S. Grant busted out of Chattanooga; General Braxton Bragg's Tennessee Army was holding it under siege. This happened in November 23-25. Under General U.S. Grant, the boys in blue were a different army. He kept drinking whiskey and smoking cigars, but the men knew he was giving them victories at last. They had confidence and charged out of Chattanooga without orders. They screamed Chickamauga, Chickamauga, to avenge their defeat there. A delighted Union yelled, "My God, come see um run!"

The Confederates wanted to hang on until the election where in all opinions Lincoln would be defeated and a pro-peace President would be elected and let the South go.

It was winter and the Armies would take a break and go into winter quarters. General Lee knew come spring they would come calling again. General Lee had to hold on to the Land of Dixie until November 1864 and pray for Abe Lincoln to be ran out of the White House.

Abe Lincoln rewarded General Grant by giving him command of the whole Union Army and General Sherman command of the western theater. This happened on March 9, 1864.

Colonel Alexander Phipps was back in uniform and it was different. This time he had the insignia of a General and he was placed in command in the weary Longstreet corps under General Pickett.

General Alexander Phipps trained his men and kept their spirits high that winter. He also sent many letters to Hagers Town to a Mrs. Henrietta Hannah Wright Adams. How many letters made it to her we will never know because they had to pass through the lines of war. He also used the name Alexander Phipps with no hint of being in the Confederate Army. He knew the Yankees would intercept the mail and even read it so he had to be silent on matters of war.

Back in Hagerstown, Hannah lived for the arrival of his letters. Even Ginger would ask Cousin Hannah how he was and what he wrote in his letters. Hannah kept it generic and never let her read a word. Hannah trusted Ginger about as much as she would a fox in the henhouse.

Hannah writes letters to her love.

May 4, 1864 was the beginning of a massive campaign by all the Union Army. General Grant takes his 120,000 man Army and marches towards Richmond. General Lee gathers his 62,000-man army and heads out to defend the land of Dixie as best as he can.

There will be three hard fought battles in the summer of 1864. The Battle of the Wilderness May 5-6, then on to Spotsylvania, on May 8-12, Then General Lee sets a trap for Grant in Cold Harbor. This time the Army of Northern Virginia built a zigzag breastwork with logs, earth, and rocks. General Grant sent in his Army in a head on frontal attack. It was murder; the confederates killed 7,000 Union soldiers in ten minutes. To make it worse Grant did not call a truce to gather the wounded and dead. They lay there in the June heat for three days. The bodies swelled up and even the hogs came out of the woods and ate on the poor Union dead. Both sides were ashamed, mostly of the hard headedness of Grant to win no matter how many men he killed. This one battle would be in the minds of the soldiers the rest of their lives. It was said that one Union soldier predicted his death and wrote in his diary, "June 3, 1864, Cold Harbor, Virginia I was killed."

In the western theater of the war, General William T. Sherman was given the command of the United States 100,000-man army and would face the Confederate General Joseph H. Johnston's 60,000 man Army.

General Alexander Phipps has seen enough bloodshed to last the lifetime of 100 men. He holds on to the memories of Hannah and the dream of being back with her. Letters were few and far between, but he cherished each word that Hannah had written.

General Grant tries to skirt around the Army of Northern Virginia and cut the railroads in Petersburg. General Lee directed his army to double time to cut off the Union Army. He told them to trot like horses or all would be lost. On June 15, 1864, the bigger stronger Union Army failed to capture Petersburg, which would result in a nine-month siege. There never has been an army like the Army of Northern Virginia. They believed so strongly in defending their homes and families they would not just give up.

General Lee had his army dig in and build trenches and bunkers; still in hopes that Abe Lincoln would be defeated in the November election of 1864. Democrat and ex-commander of the Union Army, George B. McClellan was running on the pro-peace platform.

General Alexander Phipps was so proud of his rag-tag army fighting so strongly against twice their numbers.

Battle of Cold Harbor. June 3, 1864.

Frontal Attack of the Union against the Confederates of Cold Harbor. Even General U.S. Grant admitted that was his biggest mistake of the war. Seven thousand Union Soldiers died in ten minutes. This was the last major battle the Southern Army won. Other than Battle of the Crater.

Chapter 22

The Siege Mine

During the Civil War, Petersburg, Virginia, was an important railhead, where four railroad lines from the south met before continuing to Richmond, Virginia, the capital of the Confederacy. Most of the supplies to Lee's army and to the city of Richmond funneled through this point. Consequently, the Union regarded it as the "back door" to Richmond, without which defending the Confederate capital would be impossible. The result was the Siege of Petersburg (which was actually trench warfare rather than a true siege), in which the armies were aligned along a series of fortified positions and trenches more than 20 miles long, extending from the old Cold Harbor battlefield near Richmond to areas south of Petersburg.

After Lee held at bay Grant's attempt to seize Petersburg on June 15, the battle settled into a stalemate. Grant had learned a hard lesson at Cold Harbor about attacking Lee in a fortified position and was chafing at the inactivity to which Lee's trenches and forts had confined him. Finally, Lt. Col. Henry Pleasants, commanding the 48th Pennsylvania Infantry of Maj. Gen. Ambrose E. Burnside's IX Corps, offered a novel proposal to break the impasse.

Pleasants, a mining engineer from Pennsylvania in civilian life, proposed digging a long mine shaft underneath the Confederate lines and planting explosive charges directly underneath a fort in the middle of the Confederate First Corps line. If successful, this would not only kill all the defenders in the area, it would also open a hole in the Confederate defenses. If enough Union troops filled the breach quickly enough and drove into the Confederate rear area, the Confederates would not be able to muster enough force to drive them out, and Petersburg might fall. Burnside, whose reputation had suffered from his 1862 defeat at the Battle of Fredericksburg and his poor performance earlier that year at the Battle of Spotsylvania Court House, gave permission to proceed.

Mine Construction under the Confederates.

Digging began in late June, but even Grant and Major General George Meade saw the operation as, "A mere way to keep the men occupied," and doubted it of any actual strategic value. They quickly lost interest and Pleasants soon found himself with few materials for his project, to the extent that his men had to forage for wood to support the structure. Work progressed steadily, however. Earth was removed by hand and packed into improvised sledges made from cracker boxes fitted with handles, and the floor, wall, and ceiling of the mine were shored up with timbers from an abandoned wood mill and even from tearing down an old bridge.

The shaft was elevated as it moved toward the Confederate lines to make sure moisture did not clog up the mine, and fresh air was pumped in via an ingenious air-exchange mechanism near the entrance. The miners had constructed a ventilation shaft located well behind Union lines, and connected it to the mine with canvas, which isolated the mine from outside air. At the shaft's base, a fire was kept continuously burning. Meanwhile, a wooden duct ran the entire length of the tunnel and protruded into the outside air. The fire heated stale air inside of the tunnel, forcing it up the ventilation shaft and out of the mine. The resulting vacuum then sucked fresh air in from the mine entrance via the wooden duct, which carried it down the length of the tunnel to the location where the miners were working. This precluded the need for additional ventilation shafts that could have been observed by the enemy, and served well in disguising the diggers' progress.

On July 17, the main shaft reached under the Confederate position. Rumors of a mine construction soon reached the Confederates, but Lee refused to believe or act upon it for two weeks before commencing countermining attempts, which were sluggish and uncoordinated, and were unable to discover the mine. General John Pegram, whose batteries would be above the explosion, did, however, take the threat seriously enough to build a new line of trenches and artillery points behind his position as a precaution.

The mine was in a "T" shape. The approach shaft was 511 feet long, starting in a sunken area downhill and more than 50 feet below the Confederate battery, making detection difficult. The tunnel entrance was narrow, about 3 feet wide and 4.5 feet high. At its end, a perpendicular gallery of 75 feet (23 m) extended in both directions. Grant and Meade suddenly decided to use the mine three days after it was complete after a failed attack known later as the First Battle of Deep Bottom. The Federals filled the mine with 320 kegs of gunpowder, totaling 8,000 pounds. The explosives were approximately 20 feet underneath the Confederate works and the T gap was packed shut with 11 feet of earth in the side galleries and a further 32 feet of packed earth in the main gallery to prevent the explosion blasting out the mouth of the mine. On July 28, the powder charges were armed.

Preparation for the Assault

Burnside had trained a division of United States Colored Troops (USCT) under Brig. Gen. Edward Ferrero to lead the assault. The division consisted of two brigades, one designated to go to the left of the crater and the other to the right. A regiment from each brigade was to leave the attack column and extend the breach by rushing perpendicular to the crater, while the remaining regiments were to rush through, seizing the Jerusalem Plank Road just 1,600 feet beyond, followed by the churchyard and, if possible, Petersburg itself. Burnside's two other divisions, made up of white troops, would then move in, supporting Ferrero's flanks and race for Petersburg itself. Two miles behind the front lines, out of sight of the Confederates, the men of the USCT division were trained for two weeks on the plan.

Despite this careful planning and intensive training (by Civil War standards), the day before the attack, Meade, who lacked confidence in the operation, ordered Burnside not to use the black troops in the lead assault, claiming that if the attack failed black soldiers would be killed needlessly, creating political repercussions in the North. Meade may have also ordered the change of plans because he lacked confidence in black soldiers' abilities in combat. Burnside protested to General Grant, who sided with Meade. When volunteers were not forthcoming Burnside selected a replacement white division by having the three commanders draw lots. Brig. Gen. James H. Ledlie's 1st Division was selected, but he failed to brief the men on what was expected of them and was reported during the battle to be drunk, well behind the lines, and providing no leadership. (Ledlie would be dismissed for his actions during the battle.)

Sketch of the explosion seen from the Union line.

The plan called for the mine to be detonated between

3:30 and 3:45am on the morning of July 30. Pleasants lit the fuse accordingly, but as with the rest of the mine's provisions, they had been given poor quality fuse, which his men had had to splice themselves. After more and more time passed and no explosion occurred (the impending dawn creating a threat to the men at the staging points, who were in view of the Confederate lines), two volunteers from the 48th Regiment (Lt. Jacob Douty and Sgt. Harry Reese) crawled into the tunnel. After discovering the fuse had burned out at a splice, they spliced on a length of new fuse and relit it. Finally, at 4:44 a.m., the charges exploded in a massive shower of earth, men, and guns. A crater was created, 170 feet long, 100 to 120 feet wide, and at least 30 feet deep.

The explosion immediately killed 278 Confederate soldiers, and stunned Confederate troops did not direct any significant musket or artillery fire at the enemy for at least 15 minutes. However, Ledlie's untrained division was not prepared for the explosion, and reports indicate they waited ten minutes before leaving their own entrenchments. Footbridges were supposed to have been placed to allow them to quickly cross their own trenches, but these were missing, meaning the men had to climb in and out of their own trenches just to reach no-man's land. Once they had wandered to the crater, instead of moving around it as the black troops had been trained to do, they thought it would make an excellent rifle pit and it would be well to take cover. Therefore, they moved down into the crater itself, wasting valuable time while the Confederates, under

Brig. Gen. William Mahone, gathered as many troops together as they could for a counterattack. In about an hour's time, they had formed up around the crater and began firing rifles and artillery down into it, in what Mahone later described as a "turkey shoot". The plan had failed, but Burnside, instead of cutting his losses, sent in Ferrero's men. Now faced with considerable flanking fire, they also went down into the crater, and for the next few hours, Mahone's soldiers, along with those of Maj. Gen. Bushrod Johnson and artillery, slaughtered the IX Corps as it attempted to escape from the crater. Some Union troops eventually advanced and flanked to the right beyond the Crater to the earthworks and assaulted the Confederate lines, driving the Confederates back for several hours in hand-to-hand combat. Mahone's Confederates conducted a sweep out of a sunken gully area about 200 yards) from the right side of the Union advance. This charge reclaimed the earthworks and drove the Union force back towards the east.

In later stages of the battle, many Union casualties were black soldiers killed by Confederate bayonets and musket fire. It was an insult to the Confederates to face Negro soldiers.

Crater with Union soldier in 1865.

Union casualties were 3,798 (504 killed, 1,881 wounded, 1,413 missing or captured), Confederate 1,491 (361 killed, 727 wounded, 403 missing or captured). Many of the Union losses were suffered by Ferrero's division of the USCT. Both the black and white wounded prisoners were taken to the Confederate hospital at Poplar Lawn in Petersburg. Meade brought charges against Burnside, and a subsequent court of inquiry censured Burnside along with Brig. Gens. Ledlie, Ferrero, Orlando B. Willcox, and Col. Zenas R. Bliss. Burnside was never again assigned to duty. Although he was as responsible for the defeat as Burnside, Meade escaped immediate censure. However, in early 1865, the Congressional Joint

Committee on the Conduct of the War exonerated Burnside and condemned Meade for changing the plan of attack (which did little good for Burnside, whose reputation was ruined). As for Mahone, the victory, won largely due to his efforts in supporting Johnson's stunned men, earned him a lasting reputation as one of the best young generals of Lee's army in the war's last year.

Grant wrote to Chief of Staff Henry W. Halleck, "It was the saddest affair I have witnessed in this war." He also stated to Halleck that "Such an opportunity for carrying fortifications I have never seen and do not expect again to have."

Pleasants, who had no role in the battle itself, received praise for his idea and the execution thereof. When he was appointed a brevet brigadier general on March 13, 1865, the citation made explicit mention of his role.

Grant subsequently gave in his evidence before the Committee on the Conduct of the War:

General Burnside wanted to put his colored division in front, and I believe if he had done so it would have been a success. Still I agreed with General Meade as to his objections to that plan. General Meade said that if we put the colored troops in front (we had only one division) and it should prove a failure, it would then be said and very properly, that we were shoving these people ahead to get killed because we did not care anything about them. But that could not be said if we put white troops in front."

Despite the battle being a tactical Confederate victory, the strategic situation in the Eastern Theater remained unchanged. Both sides remained in their trenches and the siege continued.

Chapter 23
Alex Goes on Furlough

The fall is coming and now the men are all building log huts for the winter and all trying to keep their heads down. Yankee sharpshooters are always looking for a gray clad Confederate target.

**Rendition of General Alexander Phipps in his new Uniform.
Notice his worriedness from the strains of war.**

Now General, Alexander Phipps would help with the preparations for winter. General Grants Army had the Confederate Army surrounded on three sides so the Confederates had to keep the other western side open for supplies and escape if that had to be objective.

This was a completely new kind of warfare, trenches and bunkers. If the Confederates kept supplies coming in they could hold out here until after the election in the North. They would have access to firewood, and food if there were any to be had. I say this because the breadbasket of the south was diminishing due to the fighting in Shenandoah Valley and from Atlanta Georgia.

The Yankees were tearing up every railroad that they could, they took up the rails and laid them in big fires. By doing this, the iron would be softened and the red-hot iron was bent into twisted messes so they could never be put back in as railroad rails.

September 2nd 1864 General Sherman's Union Army captured Atlanta thus cutting off supplies to the north. This news bolstered Abe Lincoln's chances in the election.

October 19, Union General Philip Sheridan had a big victory over Confederate General Jubal Earley in the Shenandoah Valley.

To make matters worse, the election on November 8, 1864 put Lincoln back in the White House and the Democrat and anti-war candidate, George B. McClellan was beaten. This was very bad news for the South. President Jefferson Davis and General Lee would now be forced to rethink their strategy, but no giving up and surrendering was voiced just yet.

If Lee could keep his men fed some way and in the spring join up with General Johnston's' army and go into the mountains of Virginia and North Carolina they could keep the fight up for years.

News came from Atlanta that General Sherman was applying the new method of war as the Scotched Earth method. Sherman was making a 50-mile wide swipe from Atlanta to Savannah burning homes, barns, crops, bales of hay, hemp, and cotton and plundering. There were many mentions of rape and killing. The sentiments in the south was that the atrocities committed by Sherman's Army was inhumane and infidelity.

General Lee sent for General Phipps and asked him to go north again to sniff out any information and go see your lady friend. General Phipps got himself a suit of civilian clothes and snuck out to the west. It was the only option he had to get out of the siege area of Grant's massive army. He rode Prancer through the lines and headed

north through the Shenandoah Valley towards
Hagerstown.

General Phipps was worn down from the wounds and
stress of war. He needed to get some rest and really
needed to see his Hannah.

The Yankees stopped him before he could get out of
Virginia and he would have to perform some realistic
acting to get free. He finally convinced them he was a
businessman with his old catalog and some old orders
that he had taken.

Next he was stopped by a rough looking bunch of
Confederate state guard. They seemed to be more
scavengers than soldiers. They had in mind to do him
harm and rob him, but he told them who he was and got
his papers out of his boot so they could prove his loyalty.
They let him go and wished him luck.

Finally, Alex got close to Hagerstown and the ravages of
war brought him instant memories of his last visit. He so
hoped that the Adams Family had not been molested
and his sweet Hannah was safe.

Prancer carried his worried rider to the Adams
plantation and right up to the porch. He could see the
smoke from the winter fires swirling from the chimneys.
Old Black George, the Stable man came to him and
greeted him. Alex turned Prancer over to George and he

went to the door and knocked. It was a cold dark December day now and not much going on outdoors.

Opening the door was the beautiful Hannah and when she saw Alex, she leaped on his neck almost knocked him to the ground. After she finally turned him loose, she noticed he had a beard, and looked to be so tired.

"My Darling, you look so different with your beard, and you look so frazzled, Are you alright?" asked Hannah.

"Yes I am fine, it has been rough on the army and I hurt for them," he answered.
"Well get in here and I will get you some tea and we can catch up," said Hannah.
"That sounds good, oh! Hello William," said Alex as he saw William Adams coming to greet him.

After the hugs and small talk they had supper, then the Adams' and Alex went to the parlor. One subject that came up quickly was the state of the Confederacy. It looked like the new nation was crumbling. The grand army of General Lee was under siege at Petersburg. The hopes of Lincoln being beaten is dashed as well as the hopes of the South. General Lee will do well just to keep his army fed this winter. The Confederate Nation has gone from the forth-richest nations to one of the poorest in less than four years.

Alex noticed that William Adams had a different demeanor as they talked. As the ladies sipped on some wine William and Alex sipped on some corn liquor. William has had several big drinks by now so he takes over the conversation.

He was soft spoken but to the point. He asked Hannah and Alex if they were in love. Alex looks at Hannah and Hannah looks back at Alex with love in their eyes. They both would answer but Alex answered first realizing that William was looking straight at him.

"Yes, Sir, I love Hannah with all my heart," answered Alex.

Hannah spoke out with no hesitation, "Father, I love Alex so much!"

Martha sat there listening to the profound answers with great interest.

William Adams spoke directly and without reservations, "Well, it is time for a wedding and the sooner the better."

Alex spoke up, "Well, we were waiting for the war to be over Sir."

Martha spoke up, "We know not what tomorrow will bring, seize the time you have and marry soon"
Hannah sat there all smiles and Alex kneeled down in front of her.

"Sweet Henrietta, will you marry me and be my loving wife?" asked Alex?

Next, William, Martha, and Alex focused their eyes and ears on Hannah.

"I will marry you, General Alexander Phipps and be your loving wife until I breathe my last breath," answered Hannah in the sweetest voice.

"Well now that is out of the way we can plan a wedding and the sooner the better!" exclaimed William Adams.

Martha looked at William, and said, "Tomorrow you and Alex can go to the court house and get the marriage bond and license and see the Reverend Tom Bellamy."

"Yes Mother we will do that, you can get the word out and get things ready. I think Saturday will be a grand day for the wedding since it is Christmas Day," answered William.

Alex wanted it, but felt rushed into this wedding. Then Hannah held his face and kissed him right on the lips in the presence of her father and mother. This took away any reluctance he may harbor.

Other subjects came up and right out of the blue, William asked Alex if he remembered his niece Ginger? Alex kinda stuttered when he answered. Oh! Yes, sir what about her he inquired?

"Well it seems she got in the family way and married, William Randolph Perkins," said William.

 Before William thought he said, "That woman is beautiful; bet that is not the first man she has been with."

"William, you shouldn't talk like that," said Martha.

Alex wondered, could this new baby possible be his. Then he felt relief as Ginger was safely married and he would be soon.

After all was quiet in the house that night, Hannah slipped over to visit Alexander in his room. She wore only a thin worn nightshirt even though it was cool in the house. Her pert breast were pushing against the garment and her hard nipples stood out in the pale lamp light. She was simply beautiful in the glimmering light.

Alex had on his long nightshirt. He had just been up adding wood to the fire in his fireplace so that it would be cozy when Hannah arrived. When he saw, Hannah come through the door and the light strike her beautiful figure he instantly became aroused and his member began to swell.

They stood and kissed while holding each other tightly. Then Hannah lifted the long nightshirt over his shoulders and he was completely naked. Then Alex did likewise and lifted her thin nightshirt off her.

Now two hot loving bodies embraced and Alex could feel her hot breast against his chest and her nipples burned his skin. Hannah now felt his hot hard member pressing against her soft belly. They both pulled as tight as they could.

Alex said, "Hannah, I love thee!"

Hannah responded by saying, "General Phipps, I truly love you and tonight you can have it all!"
Alex picked her up in such a loving way and carried her over to the bed. He gently laid her down and in the dim flickering light of the lamps and fireplace, he was stunned at her beauty.

The room was cool because of the cold winter temperatures outside the windows.

He got in the feather bed with her, pulled up a thick quilt, and took her into his arms.

They lay there kissing as the featherbed warmed up and soon they were warm. Hannah crawled on top of Alex keeping the quilt on them. Hannah felt so good to Alex with her hot nipples against him and the sweet kisses flowed like honey.

Alex took a nipple in both hands and pinched them gently between his fingers. He was as hard as a rock and Hannah's hot treasure was oozing out the sweet nectar of love.

"Oh! Darling I want all of you," said Hannah.

Hannah spread her legs more took her hand and placed his hard organ between the lips of her loving treasure. Alex pushed slightly, his manhood slid in, and they both moaned with pleasure.

Hannah began to move her luscious hips and her treasure was eating him alive.

"Oh my God, what a wonder you are", Alex said.

Hannah wanted more control and she wanted him deeper into her hot juicy cavity of love so she pulled her knees forward. Now she was sitting straight up and he was deep into her. Her pert breast were in his reach so he took a nipple in the fingers of each hand.

They were so hot and excited; Hannah began to rock faster and as she gyrated on his strong pole, she had an unexpected blasting orgasm and almost screamed. This brought on a blast from him as he ejaculated into her and she could feel the hot love juice shooting with each throb.

Do not worry the love birds are far from finished this night.

After they both lay there for a minute catching their breath, they both exchanged many sweet words, then without any notice, Hannah raised off him and turned around. She began to lick and suck his softening pole and cleaning him up. Her hot dripping treasure was just above his face. He took her beautiful hips in his hands, pulled her down on his mouth, and he began sucking their mixed juices and both moaned with pleasure.

After his member had once again reached its full girth, he pushed her off him, laid her down on the bed, spread her long beautiful legs and lay down on her.

Alex was now fully in charge and he pushed his hardness deep inside her and began humping her as he kissed her face all over.

Now Hannah surprised Alex by pleading to him. "Oh Darling, fuck me hard!" Someway that slang word turned Alex into a madman and he became as a loving machine."

They both thought they left this world and flew through the sky and back to earth. This time the love session lasted a long time until Hannah screamed out with a violent orgasm. Alex tried to quieten her by placing his mouth on hers and then it was his turn. Another plunge into her and he went off with a long lasting ejaculation that almost made him pass out.

They both laid there engaged until both got their breaths and she said, "Mister Phipps, I love your loving, but I better get to my bed."

At that point, Alex was so relaxed he could hardly move, so she kissed him, put on her nightshirt and slipped back to her room.

They were both in their own beds and warm. They both fell into a deep sleep and the morning was there in what seem less than an hour of joyful sleep. They both felt between their legs reminiscing of the joy of last night.

It was Wednesday morning and Saturday was coming quickly. This Day William and Alexander Phipps will go to the courthouse and get the marriage bond and license, then swing by and ask the preacher to come on Saturday.

Rendition of Hannah's Bedroom

Chapter 24
The Wedding

Saturday, (Christmas Day) came quickly and without the loving couple touching each other for three nights. They had decided to save themselves for three nights. Ha! Yes, I laughed also.

With the war going on and so many mixed emotions in the State of Maryland, there was not much in the way of the Christmas spirit. There would be Christmas services at the local churches and some would pray for peace, some for the North and some for the South.

William had gone the bond for Hannah and paid for the marriage license and then Alex and William stopped by to see the Reverend Thomas Bellamy. Brother Bellamy told them he could officiate the wedding long as he could get to the church by 6 PM for the Christmas service.

The wedding was planned for 1:30 PM and this should work for all. As promised, the Reverend Bellamy was there on time and folks were gathering in the spacious living room of the Adam's home.
Martha and Hannah had decided to keep the wedding small, so only close friends and some kin were invited. Archibald and Mary Jane Adams would be there, Mr. and

Mrs. William Randolph Perkins would be there and the Mrs. Ginger was showing at six months.

The John Livingston family were there, as well as a few other neighbors. The house was decorated mostly for Christmas. The table and the sideboard was filled with fine china and crystal with plenty of nuts, drinks and candies, and of course a wedding cake.
Up to, face the Reverend.

At 1:30 sharp, the Reverend Bellamy and General Alexander Phipps stood together. The fiddler played the wedding march and William escorted his beautiful daughter Henrietta Adams Wright up to face the reverend.

Reverend Thomas Bellamy spoke up and broke the silence, "Who gives this woman unto marriage?

William Adams had Hannah face Alex and said, "I do, her mother and I."

Then William went back and took a seat by Martha who had already started crying.

William whispered to Martha, "Now dear this is a happy occasion wipe those tears away."

Martha looked and William and smiled.

The Reverend went through a beautiful ceremony with the couple and finally said the magic words, "I present you to Mr. and Mrs. Alexander Phipps.

When Alex and Hannah faced the onlookers Alex noticed Ginger's face was red and big tears streamed down her face so he took his eyes off her quickly.

After some dancing and gay times, the folks began to leave so they could go to Christmas service at the church.

William had Alex and Hannah sit in the parlor and with Martha and while they sipped some fine wine he stood before them and had an official looking document in his hand.

Next William said, "Alex and Hannah, your mother and I have a wedding present for you and he read the document to them.

It was the deed to 100 acres of land with a fine cottage and several out buildings including a barn. It even mentioned a fine limestone well by the back porch.

Hannah knew this property and she began to cry with joy.

"Oh! Father and Mother, thank you so much this is the best gift we could ever have," said Hannah in a sweet low voice.

Alex smiled from ear to ear and politely said, "Thank Y'all I am overwhelmed."
William went on to explain that the ground was good and a hill on the back with virgin timber would shield them from the winds. He told Alex about the good little cottage and the outbuildings.

Then Martha spoke up telling them that the cottage was cleaned, furnished and stocked with food and that the slave woman, Jenny was pleased to keep the fires burning and all was ready for them.

After hugs and jesters of love between the four, William told them that, the Negro George was waiting in the carriage to deliver them to their new home.

Oh! What a happy day for Hannah and Alex. They put on their greatcoats and gathered their carpetbags, and saddlebags; the bags were filled with necessaries. They said good-bye, went out, and got in the awaiting carriage. There was even a quilt to pull up on them to ward off the winter night's cold air.

Old George greeted them and asked if they were ready to go to the Phipps farm? Alex spoke up, "Yes George, please take us to the Phipps farm."

"Yes Sir, Master Phipps I will carries y'all to youse new hoouse!"

Then he looked at Hannah with a wide smile and kissed her as the horses moved into their harnesses and the carriage was moving.

The horses were glad to get to moving as it was cold standing and waiting and they had the carriage to the cottage in short time.

Alex had never seen the farm or cottage so he was excited because Hannah was. He was thrilled that they had their own little farm with a fine little cottage and all that they needed.

George set out the weight that held the reigns to keep the lead horse stationary and then came around to get the baggage. Alex picked up his bride and carried her to the door and Jenny opened it. He carried Hannah across the threshold into their new home.

Jenny spoke up and said, "Welcome too yawls wonderful home!"

Forbidden Passion

"Thank you Jenny," said Hannah.

"Youse so welcome," answered Jenny.

"Oh! Master Phipps you have youse fine hoss and a cow, and some chickens in your barn," said Jenny.

"One moor thing I gots to tells y'all, I will be back tomorrow and be youse house servant," Master William give me to youse.

"Will you like that Jenny?" asked Hannah?

"Shurres will, I wills serve youse good," answered Jenny as she headed to the door to give the newlyweds a night of complete privacy.

Ole George told Jenny that there sure would be a hot time in the Phipps's house tonight. Jenny laughed aloud.

Ole George and Jenny went back to the big house and left Alex and Hannah to enjoy their wedding night. They were in such bliss until Alex reminded Hannah that he had to return to duty the day after New Year's Day. He would have to go to Petersburg and help General Lee all he could to preserve the Confederacy.

Hannah said, "Hush Darling, for now you are all mine."

Alex agreed and held Hannah tightly.

Then he had an urge and wonder where the Privy was. Alex told Hannah to get ready for bed he was going to run out to the little house.   She said, "Wait I will go!"

They took a candle lantern and trudged out to the outhouse. Alex noticed a light in the distance and asked Hannah what it was. She told him it was where William and Ginger Perkins live. The subject dropped. They laughed and had fun the whole time then finally got back into the warm house after taking turns on the one-hole in their privy.

Now it was time for the newlyweds to enjoy their wedding night. Alex popped the cork on a bottle of wine that was sitting on the table with two wine glasses. He poured wine into both glasses until they were about half full. Then he handed one to Hannah and proposed a toast.

"To my wife and to our marriage, may it always be happy and may we always be of one mind and endure all that life will bring us," said Alex.

They both took a drink then they kissed. Then he gently took off her top and dress. Then they kissed. She stood there in her pantaloons with her beautiful breast standing out like wonderful twin fawns.

218

Hannah helped Alex loose his shirt and pants and once again, they kissed and had another drink of wine. He had on only his drawers and a bulge had appeared. Hannah sat on a dining room chair, pulled Alex close, released his hard organ, and kissed it on the head. They had another drink and kiss. Then unexpectedly Hannah dipped her fingers in the wine, wet the head of his hard member, and then licked it off. Then she did it again and this time she took him into her mouth and sucked it dry. She raised her head, he leaned over and kissed her lips, and he stuck his tongue into her mouth. She returned the jester by giving him her tongue.

Alex straightened up again and Hannah once again applied the dipping wine to his hard member and sucked it dry. Then she took off his drawers and enjoyed the view of his hardness standing erect.

Hannah enjoyed the new little game of dipping wine and licking it off then taking him deep into her mouth. Then her next move was to sit him down on a chair and she straddled him with her hot breast in his face. At this point, there was no penetration but hot juicy lips of her pussy pressing down on his hardness. He took her right nipple into his mouth and began to suck, but the other he took between his fingers and massaged it in a wonderful way.

Hannah could not stand it; she craved his hard member inside her. She raised up took his member and guided it up into her hot juicy treasure. They both moaned with pleasure.

There they were engaged as one and had not gotten past the kitchen yet.

Hannah began to work her beautiful ass and causing her love cavity to push and suck on his hard member. He had her filled deeply and she loved it. She kept up the action and they both were hot as fire with their faces red and sweaty. He began to get rougher with her nipples and it hurt so good. Alex was coming close to a climax and so was Hannah. Hannah pumped him hard and steady, he stiffened, and even his toes curled as he shot hot semen deep into her. Hannah felt the hard penis throbbing and the hot cum shooting in her and then she exploded with a great orgasm. Hannah screamed out loudly and Alex held her tight on his throbbing member.

Hannah said, "Oh! Alex I love you."

"I love you and your wonderful loving," answered Alex.

They sat there for a few minutes then Alex picked her up, she grabbed the wine and he carried her to the bed.

He grabbed the pillows and put them down in the bed. Next, he lay her beautiful ass on them, which left her treasure raised and slightly gaped open. Then he took the wine and poured some into her. Next, he got between her long legs with his face, licked her pussy, and sucked the wine from the best vessel he had ever seen.

After he had her dried up, he mounted her and penetrated her with his now hardened member. He started out slowly but as they continued to enjoy their intercourse things speeded up until they were both moaning and again Hannah screamed out with joy as she cum again. Her reaction brought him to a climax once again with much throbbing and shooting of his hot love juice deep into her.

That night they took naps holding each other then repeated their lovemaking until the sun was up high even for a December day.

The last day of December 1864, Alex and Hannah sat at the table and wrote a letter to his parents. They told them all about the wedding and the fine farm they had. They talked some about the war but tried to be positive in all they wrote. The letter was addressed to Robert and Bessie Phipps in Wise, Wise County Virginia. Alex will carry the letter across the lines and mail it in good old Virginia to have a better chance of it getting there.

They loved, talked, and simply enjoyed each other the coming week until the first day of 1865. Alex got all his things together including his loaded 44 Navy colt. He bid Hannah farewell and they both cried as Prancer carried him away. Duty called and General Alexander Phipps was going to Petersburg to suffer with the army and to somehow, help General Lee win the independence for the Confederacy.

Alexander Phipps left his beautiful bride in tears and they both vowed to write a letter a day until he was home safe with her.

As Prancer trotted away from Hannah both Alex and Hannah cried.

Chapter 25

Hard Times In Petersburg

July and August were dry and sultry; water was scarce, and hard to get at. The picket post suffered the most this way, until we sank several wells in our trenches, and then we had fair water. On out post duty we were not allowed the little shelter tents so common to both armies; as when erected, they might impede our efforts to resist a surprise of the post. Therefore, we had to sweat it out the best we could. One day a commotion amongst our neighbors in blue across the way attracted our attention; and we saw a Federal soldier speeding across the fields toward Fort Sedgewick with a

Fort Sedgwick at Petersburg – Library of Congress

number of canteens on. He was after water, and braved our shots for the precious liquid. Fire was opened on him, more on the impulse of the moment than anything else, and my friend upset him; he made several attempts to rise, but could not, and finally fell back, and lay quiet.

A few minutes afterwards we noticed a stretcher, such as used to carry off the wounded, raised from behind a pit; we knew that they wanted to go out and bring in the wounded man. We yelled to "go ahead, we won't shoot," and taking us at our word, four of them made their way out and carried the man into the pine timber around Sedgewick. While this was going on, both picket lines watched the act of humanity; and neither attempted fire upon the other, though both were greatly exposed. Life on the picket line was the same every day, varied by such incidents as these. Life in the trenches proper was burdensome; none was allowed to just sit for a long time. Huge traverses forty feet high, twelve feet thick, and one hundred feet long, were raised to catch the fire of the enemy's batteries. Day and night, we labored until the huge crib of earth was completed; and then feeling safe, we became careless and idle.

The rear of earth works were dug out and widened. Three steps or platforms carried you up to the level of the works when necessary. In this wide trench we lived; our little shelters were erected; they being so much lower than the breastworks, we felt less danger than common. Before the traverses were finished, we were greatly disturbed by a Rodman gun which had an awful fire upon us. The gun was about one mile distant and the gunners were wonderfully accurate in their shots.

We called it the "greased lightning gun," because the ball would come whistling before we heard the sound. That gun has often made us scatter as its shell came bounding in amongst our tents, camp kettles and trunks of trees. It would strike a stump, glance off at right and left angles in another direction. It often would strike something else, and go the contrary course, causing everything to get out of its way.

Yells, whoops, cat-calls, dog-barks and cheers, greeted the erratic course of these contrivances of death. It would force a hasty exit of some lazy, slumbering soldier from its path, which in itself caused merriment. One round shot came bounding down the line scattering everything; it was ricocheting and meant business. As it struck in the 12th regiment they sounded the alarm, and we cleared the way.

Confederate trench work near Petersburg

 A German in our in the trenches remained in its path to look after a pot of coffee; and in attempting to dodge, it ran plum against it; and his leg was taken off for his foolishness.

The ball stopped near us, and spun around until it was as bright as a Silver dollar. One soldier put out his foot, to see if it still had much strength or devilment in it and found out to his sorrow that it did, for it had force enough to snap his ankle; and to-day he stumps along on a wooden leg. Such was life those days in the trenches. Something of this kind was frequently happening. Bombs were bursting in the air, and the Minnie balls would brush your hair as it whizzed by.

Four years of active service had care-hardened the men; and for a time they were indifferent to all that happened. Lots of hard work finally completed the works, and we felt then almost impregnable. We never left the lines, only for a market trip to Petersburg, which we still owned. Provisions were too high for us to buy; but it did seem good to see them, even if we could not buy.

Illustration of Petersburg, Virginia, from Harper's
Weekly, December 13, 1862

A common meal cost ten dollars. We fought for eleven
dollars a month. One month's hard fighting for a mess of
potatoes, and rancid meat made into a stew, and
covered with swarms of flies. Our wells furnished plenty
of water, sweeps drew it out; an ammunition box made
the bucket; a strap on a sapling made the rope; thus, we
managed. We washed our clothes in the trenches; dried
them there; ironed them there, by rubbing them around
a smooth pole; and got our fuel from the brush and
limbs in front of the works, with which to boil the

clothes, to kill the stench, and then when boiled enough the kettle would be rinsed out. In addition, any meat we could get would be boiled for rations.

One pot answered for many purposes. We rested secure. The works warded off the bullets and shells to some extent. We were numb to the shells and awaited the storm of battle to burst upon us.

In no time, all fuel close by was burned; and then details of men hauled wood some five miles to us. It was divided among each of the squads.

We dug a counter-mine toward Fort Sedgewick; but soon abandoned it; too much work for nothing so we thought.

Shells flew overhead pretty thick, and afforded a source of revenue to the poor Confederate soldier, which in those hard times was indeed a God send. Men spent time gathering iron fragments of exploded shells and the lead balls that fell behind our lines in vast quantities and selling them to the junk dealers at Petersburg, who bought them up for the C.S. Government.

It was not unusual to sight to see dozens of ragged Confederates digging, gouging, and gathering to themselves the precious fragments in heaps from the fields to our rear. Thousands of pounds of each were gathered, and disposed of at good figures; and the iron showers that burst over-head proved a blessing in this respect; and brought income to man, where it was intended to wreak destruction. The government had it worked over into shell and balls, which would be sent to us. Then we returned it to our foe to make death or be lost in the pines.

The soldiers finally became so reckless that frequently orders had to be issued forbidding the men to gather the iron.

Dozens of soldiers racing after a huge mortar shell; they knew about where it would drop, and recklessly exposed themselves to secure the shell or its pieces. These shells would frequently not burst, and this was a prize eagerly striven for, as it worth about thirty dollars.

Between our lines and Petersburg was a pond in which we had some delightful baths; but the mortar guns got the range, and broke up the fun. No one wanted to be struck while in bathing, as he would drown before help would reach him.

It was funny to see dozens of the boys hurrying out of the water, as the dull explosion told the warning to look out for shells; and they would flatten themselves naked to the ground to escape the shelling.

The ingenuity of many of the soldiers was wonderful in providing personal comforts. Two usually bunked together, one man's rations furnished the morning meal, the other the evening one.

Shoes were patched and soled with the flap of cartridge boxes taken from fields of victory. The shoes furnished by the C.S. Government were worthless.

In many instances, the leather would be green; and sometimes the hair was left on and it looked like the men had critter on their feet. In war time men find amusement where they can.

The English shoes had a thin leather sole; and the filling was of paper; they answered well enough in camp and for cavalry; but for marches they were worthless. Our clothes were of every grade, butternut pants would be patched behind with a large heart-shape patch of "Yankee blue," and contrasted funny. No full uniform was seen amongst the soldiers of the line. A store shirt was a luxury, and if a man had one it was frequently borrowed by the gallants of the regiment when they called on the fair citizens of Petersburg. (A dress up occasion) Some were course cotton with a pink plaitee or ruffled bosom. That was a shirt in those times. A blue half cotton shirt sent from home was sold in Petersburg for thirty-five dollars. Our uniforms, or what was intended for such, were of every description of material and cut.

"Prisoners from the Front," by Winslow Homer,
depicting Confederates Captured at Petersburg –
Metropolitan Museum of Art

We could not get soap, so we traded on the picket post
with the Federals. We drew an abundance of the best
tobacco, and this being scarce and dear with our
Northern friends, we could drive a bargain easy enough.

Some of the ways the Southern soldier adopted for his
personal comfort was so amusing. It showed how he
adapted himself to circumstances; and this very fact is
one of the leading reasons why the Southerner was
naturally a better soldier than the Yankees were. Most
southern men could ride, shoot and live off most
anything.

Inspections seldom occurred during the siege; but a glance was all that was necessary to see that the arms were clean, bright, and ever ready. Much trouble was had with the soldiers of Lee's army about the bayonet. The most stringent laws and punishments failed to force him to carry one. Finally, each soldier was charged up with a bayonet on the roll and if he did not have one on payday, it had to be paid for out of his hard-earned eleven dollars. These men paid more attention to the rifle, than to a cumbersome, useless weapons.

The latter days of July were characterized by intense and sultry heats. For comfort many of the boys would brave the deadly crack of the sharpshooter's rifle in order to breathe the pure, fresh air. They would hit the ponds in the rear when possible.

Such was the condition of affairs when the monotony of life in the trenches was broken by orders, the evening before July 29th, to man the entire length of the lines in our front by 4 o'clock in the morning. Having been quiet for some time before, all were of course more or less numb, so when the hour rolled by on July 30th, the most obedient only obeyed the order. Some slowly and reluctantly fell into line, and with a yawn answered "here."

Others, slept oblivious of duty, while friends answered for them, or a drowsy response came from their bunks.

Weeks of inactivity had partly relaxed discipline. Besides, they felt a consciousness that for a direct attack they had nothing to fear. The same state of affairs as regarded our strength of position prevailed with our commanders, and to the last days the judgment was sustained, as the line was never taken, but turned at Five Forks.

Daylight of July 30th dawned upon a scene of activity, and bustle in the trenches. In vain we peered into the glimmering of daylight toward our enemy for signs; all was still.

Even the picket line was very quiet; and gradually all sought easy positions and waited. Another false alarm, we thought, to try the men, and see if they were prepared for a sudden attack of the Federals on our works. To our left lay a portion of Beauregard's army; beyond him, to Appomattox River, was a part of Gordon's command. The country in front of our lines there was rough and rugged ravines, and gullies kept back most any assaulted with any certainty of success.

While we lay nodding for a few minutes against the breast-works, catching catnaps and indulging in memories of loved ones at home, someone cried out, "Look yonder!"

More about the Battle of the Crater

As we did so we saw a dark, heavy mass of matter; smoke and flame ascending high into the air, and accompanied with a rumbling noise; in an instant more it began falling. A mine had been sprung under a fort; and the order to man the lines, emanating the evening before, showed that our commander knew before hand, and had used the precaution to have his troops prepared for action.

The debris had scarcely settled before every Federal gun that could be brought to bear upon the ruptured lines opened a terrific bombardment. We crouched close to our works to escape the fury of the storm of projectiles, and feeling secure, we grinned defiance. The earth shook and trembled. The air was full of racing projectiles seething, hissing and bursting overhead flinging their splinters in every direction. The din that pierced the charge of Pickett at Gettysburg was nearly equaled here, gun for gun and shot for shell and showers of iron flew everywhere. The bulk of it fell upon the exploded lines, half a mile distant to our left. We got a good share, to prevent the army from taking part in the recapture of the lines.

The seasoned soldiers knew that an assault would shortly take place, for a heavy cannon fire generally preceded an attack. We wanted it to occur in our front, for a view was opened and fully a mile wide, and we knew that the whole Federal army could not drive us. The mortar guns in the pines around Fort Sedgewick soon joined in, and began dropping their shells lively, and most too accurately; some inside the works, some behind, and one fell right on top of the slope, tearing a deep hole, and covering everyone around with dirt.

These mortar shells always created more demoralization than any other projectile. They could not be dodged. In front of the works was just as safe as the rear.

Anywhere except way back was as good as another was. In fact, for a while the front seemed the safest place.

In the midst of the combat, Gen. Mahone came down the lines and viewed with anxiety the surroundings; and gave some general orders. The General was in his fighting weight that day, ninety-seven pounds; and was clothed in a linen uniform of jacket and pants cut after a boy's pattern, and made out of the material that composed the little shelter tents provided by Uncle Sam for the comfort of the "boys in blue and grey."

He had scarcely left before orders put the division into line; and as the Alabamians moved off, we opened our ranks and covered their space, and so on until the entire length of the division was covered; and then Harris' Brigade occupied a mile or more front, and each individual stood about forty feet apart, on the day of the battle of the Crater, July 30th.

Our batteries were not idle, but kept the enemy very busy.

We awaited the signals from our left, and when the shrill cries of the attacking force came above the din, we began to feel anxious; for what could we do, one man to defend forty feet; but we relied on our batteries to break the column if it came; but fully expecting at any time the order, to "about face," and engage the enemy, as he swept up the lines.

The conflict at the Crater was raging now with fury. Cheers and yells alternately told of advantage. We knew exactly when Mahone got down working steady, regular volleys from their muskets, for his men always fought well under discipline. Our line to our rear was swarming with fugitives, many of whom we induced to remain with us and help defend the works if necessary. Others too badly demoralized to listen to duty, moved off in disregard of our begging. Many of them presented a pitiable sight as dazed, and uncertain of what had occcured, they recounted the improbabilities of the explosion. No doubt wonderful escapes were had; bordering on exaggeration, and improbable.

A tall, confederate from Carolina, in a woeful voice described to us, as he rested within our lines, of the effect of the "blow up."

He said "he was cooking coffee, having arisen early according to orders; when all at once the ground all around him heaved up, and he saw and felt the fire and heat as it rushed by him, scorching him badly; he was thrown into the air, and fell into a pile of debris, but had sense enough to keep kicking, thus warding off much of the falling earth. Beside him lay a soldier with the upper part of his body buried, his legs sticking out, and working in vain efforts to get out; his sufferings soon ended, as death by suffocation ensued."

Many poor wretches presented sickening sights, as flame scorched or powder-burnt, or crippled by heavy falls, they filed by us. Some were wild in their sufferings, and recklessly exposed themselves to the sharpshooters now doubly venomous. We did what lay in our power for their relief and wondered at this new phase of warfare.

Illustration of Union Sharpshooters at Petersburg by
Alfred Waud – LIbrary of Congress

The battle, by 7 o'clock, was going all right, and
Mahone's men had the advantage; they were driving the
blacks and whites; and as they crossed the open field we
saw the rush and fury of the battle A friend in
Weiseiger's brigade – Mahone's old command – told us
of the fight, and what he saw. "We understood through
our officers," said he, "that no quarter was to be shown
the nigger soldiers. They had shown no mercy to the

fallen Confederates; and none should be shown them. All must be killed and no prisoners must be taken."

Continuing, he said: "We formed in several columns, and then advanced to the charge; as we crossed the rise of the ridge a furious fire was poured into us from all sides, which worked us up to a high pitch of desperation and frenzy."

The idea of having to fight niggers, and seeing our comrades falling by their fire, was maddening; thus excited the men and they swept forward. Their line was easily broken, and they were driven headlong back to the main line in and around the crater.

Fighting in the Crater at Petersburg –

Among these, they plunged and sought safety in the depths of the mine and to hundreds of them proving their fear. The resistance they offered did not check our assault; the cry of "no quarter to the dam rebels!" rang out at intervals, and was answered by a shot or a stab with the bayonet at some poor devil Negro who fell into our hands.

Gradually we approached the very edge of the gap, and saw it seething with frenzied human beings; some fighting; some crying for mercy, for help; and others, "no quarter!" They struggled for room or shelter, while a shower of Minnie balls was pouring in on them; the living dying by the hands of the dead, as it were, as they fell so thick and fast, crushing and suffocating those around them.

The white Federal troops acted very cowardly, and their bullets destroyed as many Negro lives as of the Confederates. Thus between two fires the poor black soldiers soon fell to the last man; and the pit became a vast burial vault. The scene was one of demoniac conception, one never to be forgotten.

We lay down on the brink, loaded and fired our rifles into the dense mass, where every ball found a mark. One man that seemed insane with devilish impulse would gather rifles from around him, and throw them into the pit, where the dull thud told that the bayonet was driven to very shank.

A Confederate gun secure from Federal attack got the range of the mine, and threw shell and shot with frightful precision. We got tired of the slater with blood, and was glad to hear orders to retire given; and the dying were left with the dead.

The record of that day's work shows a dreadful one; full twenty-two hundred Federals were killed of whom more than eighteen hundred were Negroes. The attack was badly managed; wretchedly led; and from the first start a huge failure; and met a barrier indeed in Mahone's veterans, when they were thrown into the breach.

A portion of this fight we could see if we chose to risk butting our heads against Minnie balls, and it was frequently risked. The artillery fire upon us had not ceased; the ground around us was cratered and torn by the cannon balls. And as a sheet of Minnie balls, as it were, constantly swept just over the breast-works, singing deceptive tunes as if to lure one on to meet the danger.

In the height of the fray, while Mahone and Beauregard were charging, Gen. Lee alone and on foot, came into our lines and adjusting his glass swept the field in front for some time with some anxiety. Apparently not satisfied with the survey and to our consternation he left the protection of the works, and advanced to our open rear, and then carefully and calmly surveyed the battle-field. Point after point was carefully scanned.

Picture to yourself the tumult of battle; men frenzied by passions contending in death grapple; the very air dark with exploding material; the ringing cheers or yells of combatants; the death shriek; the wail of agony; the appeals for mercy from some poor stricken wretch, as he knows his days are numbered. The ground around torn and great furrows of dirt continually being thrown up as shot and shell strike, and in the midst of this scene stands our fearless commander, Gen. Robert E. Lee, bare headed, erect, proud and magnificent. Gracefully he sweeps the field and takes into consideration the most trivial matter.

We looked on anxiously and trembled for his safety. A shell rushing by strikes our well sweep, and hurls the fragments far to the rear. Unconscious of danger, there he stood until satisfied. Great uneasiness prevailed for fear some sharp shooter might spy him, with a fatal aim and several of the 48th regiment went to him and kindly remonstrated with him for thus exposing himself. An Irishman, who exposed himself a few steps from Gen. Lee, was shot through the head. No wonder we were so concerned for the life of our great General.

Gen. Lee kindly noticed this demonstration of affection, and soon after came back into the lines. He was interested in the many little conveniences the men had contrived for comfort, and drank a cup of water from our wells. A fireplace cut out of the bank of earth seemed to please him. With a salute peculiar only to himself, he retired; and then all felt a sense of relief, while prayers of thankfulness arose from grateful hearts for his preservation.

The battle ended; quiet was again supreme, a few shells only coursing the heavens more out of practice than with intent to harm. The day after the "mine fiasco," I obtained permission to see the battle field. It was hot as blazes, both overhead from the sun; and the more dangerous ones contrived by man for man's destruction bomb-shells. Taking a round-about way, I found myself in Blanford cemetery, where a look could be had generally of the field and of the opposing lines. Near the monument erected to the "Cockade City's," heroes of the war of 1812, I sheltered myself and took in the sights. Marks of cruel war and havoc abounded even here in the "silent city of the dead."

Great holes in the ground, deep and yawning, told that mortar shells had fallen there. Shafts and monuments rendered into many fragments spoke of the sharp rush of cannon balls; while blue spattered marks on almost every stone in the yard, many of them split and chipped,

244

showed where the Minnie ball had struck. Of the effect of these latter messengers of death, I had scrambled a few minutes later, as one came humming by and struck a simple slab, making a bluish splash and cracking the stone.

As a bomb-shell came rushing down, and exploded just overhead, wreathed in a beautiful coil of dark, dense smoke, with rattling fragments falling in every direction, I came to the conclusion that it would appear queer to be killed behind a sheltering tombstone, so I "changed my place," and sneaked my way out as quietly as if I was leaving a dead friend.

Later in the winter with the cold the men suffered from want of clothing. The wood to burn had to be carried from five to ten miles away because it had been consumed in the fires by the cold men.

Food was scares, but the frozen cabbage was a blessing as it had the vitamins that kept back scurvy.

During the real cold times, the few greatcoats in the whole army were shared with those on picket duty.

It was men like General Alexander Phipps that kept the morale on good standing. Even the officers had blue days but all knew the winter would end someday.

General Phipps thought about his love, Hannah, back in Hagerstown every day. They both wrote love letters but who knows how far they went as neither received many.

Back in Hagerstown, everything was changing to the Yankee way of thinking. Sometimes the Adams' and the Livingston's were treated differently now because they helped a Confederate Colonel. William Adams had even condoned the marriage of his daughter to that rebel. There were feuds brewing between lots of families because of their stand with one side or the other.

A hope for peace failed as Abe Lincoln met with Confederate Vice President Alexander Stephens on February 3, 1865 at Hampton Roads, Virginia. General Alexander Phipps and a small contingent of officers were with the Vice President. Abraham Lincoln had a like number of Federal Officers with him.

Lincoln would not bend one bit because he could smell the end of the war coming. Confederate Alexander Stephens was ready to give some concessions. He would not agree to come back into the Union.

Chapter 26
The Last Days

General Alexander Phipps and his bride Hannah kept in touch the best they could by letter. They were both so worried about each other and the hunger and craving for each other was almost unbearable. They both were wise enough to know it was better to stay busy.

Hannah stayed busy with work around their cottage and milking the cow every day. She even borrowed help from her father and had the fields plowed and had 200 pounds of seed potatoes planted and hilled up big to keep of the last cold spells.

Hannah was a proper Lady but she wanted to learn the simple things a regular wife did. She learned about churning the cream into butter. She learned cooking and baking.

Jenny her slave woman enjoyed the closeness with Hannah and did not hold back teaching the art of cooking.

General Alexander Phipps stayed busy with reports and the continued effort to keep the army ready to fight and in good spirits.

Back in Hagerstown, Ginger Perkins was huge now with her baby due near the end of March. She and Hannah had tea from time to time and talked about the days they played as children. Ginger never one time mentioned anything about Alex and this made Hannah wonder about her.

Ginger knew her baby belonged to Alex but she would never tell in this lifetime. William Randolph Perkins was thrilled to have this beautiful woman as his wife, but felt something was missing in their marriage at times.

William and Martha made it a point to see Hannah most every day. Martha told William that she did not think Hannah could stand to lose her second husband and prayed for Alex daily.

On March 25, 1865 General Lee decided on a preemptive strike and sent out his army against Grant's center but in four hours the Confederates retreated back to their trenches.
April 2, 1865 General Grant with a well-supplied army mounts a general advance and breaks through the Confederate line at Petersburg.

Confederate General A.P. Hill is killed. Next General Lee orders the evacuation of Petersburg and Richmond. Looting and burning is started in the streets of Richmond. The next day, March 3 1865 the union army enters Richmond and raise the flag of the United States. Confederate Congress are on the run and hope to regroup somewhere soon.

General Lee's Army of Northern Virginia are without food and have to meet a wagon train waiting for them to the east. The rains are heavy and the roads are pure mud. General Pickett knows the morale is spinning down and makes a decision that always works to inspire the men. He had them form up as on parade and pass in review in the rain and mud.

The Army had to eat something so General Lee sent out several squads to forage the lands north and south. They brought back little and this cost the army a day of travel and gave Grant's huge, well supplied, army an advantage.
General Lee needed to get to that wagon train of food and then head south to meet up with General Johnstons Army in Carolina. His hope was that with his combined armies he might trap Grant and force a surrender. It was not to be, the Yankee Army has captured the wagon train and Union General Sheridan's carvary cut through the center of Lee's march, then cut out 15,000 men and carried them off to prison.

General Lee sat on Old Traveler his famous horse, up on a little knoll observing the fight through his binoculars and said, "My God is the Army dissolved?"

Up at the point of the Army they were doing well at this point against the Yankees. General Alexander Phipps was riding and encouraging the army that he could reach.

April 8th General Lee, after talking with Longstreet and other officers decided it was time. The bloodletting was now proving useless. He was now so undermanned and undersupplied he just could not ask any more from his brave men.

General Lee sent a dispatch to General Grant asking for terms if he surrendered. Lee wanted his men to be mustered out and be free to go home. He wanted them to take their horses and mules, as they privately owned them anyway. He wanted his army to be given good rations. General Grant agreed to this and would meet General Lee at Appomattox Court House on April 9, 1865.

Many of the poor starved confederates cried because they had to give up their dream of having their own country.

That was a sad, sad day for General Lee and his army. Lee was a true gentleman so he got out his best uniform, (The only one with General insignia as he wore Colonel

Stars the whole war and rode to Appomattox Court House to meet General Grant.

Grant showed up late and had a muddy sloppy uniform on, but was a man of his word and gave Lee the concessions to end the war.

The men north and south saluted General Lee as he rode by on his old warhorse, Traveler.

General Lee told his men, *"After four years of arduous service marked unsurpassed courage and fortitude the Army of Northern Virginia has been compelled to yield to overwhelming numbers and resources."*

The men of the south were sad but proud. They obeyed General Lee and followed instructions from their foe and stacked arms and were given food and in a short time after all had taken the oath to the United States were allowed to head home. Many of the men had to be helped because of wounds, sickness, or malnutrition yet these were fortunate. Not that far away in Point

Lookout, Maryland POW camp, some men would not be freed until late June 1865.

The end has come!

The Surrender April 9 1865

Chapter 27
Alex Goes Home To Hannah

General Alexander Phipps is now Mister Alex Phipps as he travels to Hagerstown on Prancer. He is worn, mentally tired and so disheartened by the outcome of the four-year struggle. He still wears his old tattered uniform as he travels. He has no shame for fighting for what he believed to be the right cause.

His thoughts transverses to Hannah and so wants to hold her and feel the soothing touch of her body holding him.

Rendition of Hannah serving tea to Martha, Mary Jane and Mrs. Livingston.

253

He wonders and hopes beyond all hope that he will find his kin and property all well. He especially hopes that his darling Hannah is well and will greet him happily.

As Alex travels on Prancer, he passes many burned homes, barns, and even crops lay black. He see folks along the way some greet him and wave, while others look at him with scorn. He hopes that someway the country can heal and that the Yankee's will not be bitter in their victory. He knows that the Victor of any war will write the history and he fears that it will paint a picture of the south as traitors, not Patriots.

Alex was home for a short time when word came around the nation and world. Abraham Lincoln is dead. John Wilkes Booth was a well-known actor and a Confederate spy from Maryland; though he never joined the Confederate army, he had contacts with the Confederate secret service. In 1864, Booth formulated a plan (very similar to one of Thomas N. Conrad previously authorized by the Confederacy) to kidnap Lincoln in exchange for the release of Confederate prisoners.

Shown in the presidential booth of Ford's Theatre, from left to right, are Henry Rathbone, Clara Harris, Mary Todd Lincoln, Abraham Lincoln, and his assassin John Wilkes Booth. (Picture on next page.)

THE ASSASSINATION OF PRESIDENT LINCOLN

After attending an April 11, 1865, speech in which Lincoln promoted voting rights for blacks, an incensed Booth changed his plans and became determined to assassinate the president. Learning that the President, First Lady, and head Union general Ulysses S. Grant would be attending Ford's Theatre, Booth formulated a plan with co-conspirators to assassinate Vice President Andrew Johnson, Secretary of State William H. Seward and General Grant. Without his main bodyguard, Ward Hill Lamon, Lincoln left to attend the play *Our American Cousin* on April 14. Grant, along with his wife, chose at the last minute to travel to Philadelphia instead of attending the play.

Lincoln's bodyguard, John Parker, left Ford's Theater during intermission to join Lincoln's coachman for drinks in the Star Saloon next door. The now unguarded President sat in his state box in the balcony. Seizing the opportunity, Booth crept up from behind and at about 10:13 pm, aimed at the back of Lincoln's head and fired at point-blank range, mortally wounding the President. Major Henry Rathbone momentarily grappled with Booth, but Booth stabbed him and escaped.

After being on the run for 10 days, Booth was tracked down and found on a farm in Virginia, some 70 miles south of Washington, D.C. After a brief fight with Union troops, Booth was killed by Sergeant Boston Corbett on April 26.

An Army surgeon, Doctor Charles Leale, was sitting nearby at the theater and immediately assisted the President. He found the President unresponsive, barely breathing and with no detectable pulse. Having determined that the President had been shot in the head, and not stabbed in the shoulder as originally thought, he attempted to clear the blood clot, after which the President began to breathe more naturally. The dying President was taken across the street to Petersen House. After remaining in a coma for nine hours, Lincoln died at 7:22 am on April 15. Presbyterian minister Phineas Densmore Gurley, then present, was asked to offer a prayer, after which Secretary of War Stanton saluted and said, "Now he belongs to the ages."

The South knew they were in for even harder time when they heard the news of the Presidents' death. Lincoln was talking about a good operation of bringing all the Confederate States back into the Union. Now there would be punishments administered to pay back the South.

Even in the Union Prisoner of War camps, the men would be treated worse and be held for months after the surrender of General Lee. The commander at Point Lookout Prisoner of War Pen rode his big-footed horse in between the poor starving Confederates as they sat talking and picking off lice.

What else can go wrong for Alex and Hannah as they try to start a life after the war? At least the State of Maryland had been stopped from succeeding by the Federal Government and now would not be receiving the harsh treatment of the Federal Government.

Now that Alex was home with Hannah they could forget the world in their wonderful sessions of love. They do know they cannot live on love, but it is a great way to block out the pain of the war and after effects.

The day Alex rode in, Hannah was working in her vegetable garden when she saw him coming out of the corner of her eye. She threw down her hoe, ran to him, and grabbed the harness of Prancer and he pulled up short giving Alex a sudden stop. He jumped down, they hugged so tight, and she kissed him all over his face, even the bearded part.

Prancer just stood there though he was unattended and seemed to enjoy the greeting his master was receiving. Then Alex took his saddlebags and gear to the porch, kissed Hannah one more time and headed to the barn. In those days, a man did not neglect his horse. His horse was a friend and his transportation. A horse could be the difference between life and death in some events. After Alex seen to the needs of Prancer, he came into their cottage and there was Hannah with the bathing tub set out and water heating in the fireplace.

Next thing Hannah was dishing him out some stew and had a biscuit left from breakfast. In these days, this was quick food.

Alex sat down and Hannah helped him pull off his knee high riding boots. His boots were well worn and his socks were full of holes. His once elegant uniform was tattered and soiled with the dirt of battle. This condition of his uniform was mild to the average private. The private's uniforms were all mixed in color and well worn. Most had patches all over or open holes. Most uniforms were mere rags and the stench of war and death hang in the fibers.

Forbidden Passion

Hannah had on a cotton day dress and the once bright colors were now faded and worn. She still had a couple of beautiful ball gowns in her trunk, but had no reason to wear them as late.

Hannah could not keep her hands off her beloved husband and Alex enjoyed touching her body. As he sat he pulled her to his lap and they kissed, then he let his hands find her breast. They could not wait until baths were over, so he reached under her skirt and pulled down her panties and she opened his pants and she straddled him in the chair. His member was swelled and hard and the lips of her treasure went around him as she sat on him. He went in deep and they both moaned with the much-needed pleasure. Soon Hannah was bobbing up and down and he had her top opened and had a nipple in his hand and the other in his mouth trying to hold on as she moved up and down with his member rubbing her clitoris. They both moaned and all of a sudden, there was a quickening in him and her as he exploded with a powerful ejaculation and she followed almost instantly with a powerful organism.

She sat there for a long time, as they loved on each other. Then unexpected Hannah informed him that he was going to be a father. He was shocked, but instantly thrilled at the idea. She was almost four months pregnant from their Christmas honeymoon. They were so happy even though the cause of the fight was lost.

Much loving went on after supper and baths. He helped her with her bath and she helped him. All of this was so important to the young but worn couple. Now they had something to look forward to and things to plan for.

A black servant girl came the very next day to fetch Hannah for Ginger. Ginger was in a stressful labor and needed help. Hannah rushed to help after a quick kiss from Alex.

Alex wondered, what if that baby was his, it was in the right time frame. It must remain a secret and he should stay away from Mrs. Ginger Perkins even though she had basically ran off her husband. William Randolph Perkins was staying with his parents not far away.

Think about all of this. Hannah is happy to have her man back home and they are going to have a new baby Phipps.

Ginger is having a baby and she hates her husband, as he is not the lover Alex is.

William Randolph loves the beautiful Ginger and thinks the baby belongs to him.

I think there will be much more to tell as time goes on.

Information

To see other books published by "Dahnmon Whitt Family Publishing," go to Amazon.com or to the web site at http://dahnmonwhittfamily.com/

Lucy Elizabeth "Liz" Fleming wants to remain anonymous. However, watch out she may have more hot Historic-Romance novels coming your way.